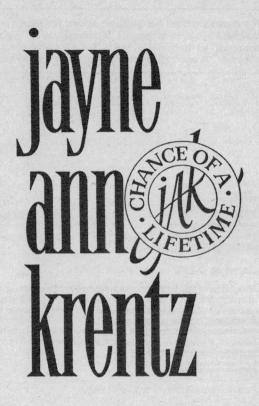

jayne ann krentz

CHANCE OF A · LIFETIME

Harlequin Books

TORONTO • NEW YORK • LONDON
AMSTERDAM • PARIS • SYDNEY • HAMBURG
STOCKHOLM •ATHENS• TOKYO • MILAN
MADRID • WARSAW • BUDAPEST • AUCKLAND

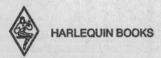 **HARLEQUIN BOOKS**

CHANCE OF A LIFETIME

Copyright © 1987 by Jayne Ann Krentz

All rights reserved. Except for use in any review, the reproduction or utilization of this work in whole or in part in any form by any electronic, mechanical or other means, now known or hereafter invented, including xerography, photocopying and recording, or in any information storage or retrieval system, is forbidden without the written permission of the publisher, Harlequin Enterprises Limited, 225 Duncan Mill Road, Don Mills, Ontario, Canada M3B 3K9.

ISBN: 0-373-83318-0

First Harlequin Books printing August 1987

Reprinted July 1994

All characters in this book have no existence outside the imagination of the author and have no relation whatsoever to anyone bearing the same name or names. They are not even distantly inspired by any individual known or unknown to the author, and all incidents are pure invention.

This edition published by arrangement with Harlequin Enterprises B. V.

® and TM are trademarks of the publisher. Trademarks indicated with ® are registered in the United States Patent and Trademark Office, the Canadian Trade Marks Office and in other countries.

Printed in U.S.A.

jayne ann krentz

One of today's top contemporary romance writers, Jayne Ann Krentz has an astounding twelve million copies of her books in print. Her novels regularly appear on the *New York Times,* Waldenbooks and B. Dalton bestseller lists. First published in 1979, Jayne quickly established herself as a prolific and innovative writer. She has delved into psychic elements, intrigue, fantasy, historicals and even futuristic romances.

Jayne lives in Seattle with her husband, Frank, an engineer, and her bird, Ferd, whom she modestly refers to as "a truly brilliant budgie."

1

RACHEL WILDER HAD LEARNED in recent weeks that revenge was a strange and consuming passion. It was insidious. It was devious. It did not explode into life; rather, it began as a stray, wistful thought, a fleeting desire that did not quite dissolve, even though one told oneself it was impossible to pursue. It hung around in one's mind, feeding on other emotions such as frustration and anger, all the while growing larger and more important.

It wasn't long, Rachel had discovered to her grim shock, before the desire for revenge overcame not only the softer emotions but common sense, as well.

Surely only the destruction of her normal common sense could explain her presence here in the rugged foothills of California's Sierra Nevada. She must be as crazy as any of the miners who had once streamed into these hills searching for gold. The odds of finding revenge or even a satisfying confrontation with the man who had caused her stepsister such anguish were probably on a par with striking it rich. About a million to one.

But she had to try. The habit of protecting Gail Vaughan was too strong, too ingrained to allow Rachel to ignore the situation. Gail had always been such a delicate, sensitive child, at least according to her mother. She had been deeply affected by the loss of her own father at an early age, and her mother had worried terribly about her young daughter. It was an attitude Rachel herself had quickly adopted when her new stepmother and stepsister moved into the home Rachel and her father had shared since the death of Rachel's mother. Rachel had been so eager to please her new relations that she'd been more than willing to slip into the role of protective older sister. Protecting Gail had become a habit, a habit Gail often found useful.

Rachel loved her stepsister, but she wasn't totally blind to the fact that somewhere along the way, Gail had gotten spoiled. She was a very lovely young woman who had learned early on that people found her waiflike vulnerability charming. Even Rachel wasn't sure just how strong her stepsister really was. No one had ever put Gail's strength to the test.

The habit of taking care of Gail was hard to shake; Rachel's sense of responsibility went deep. It was now instinctive for her to fight the battles her stepsister always seemed to find so overwhelming. Over the years there had been a number of such battles.

Occasionally Rachel suspected Gail enjoyed the luxury of being able to turn her problems over to someone else to solve. There were moments when it occurred to her that Gail had gotten very good at relying on her older sister, moments when it seemed that Gail had learned to use her feisty stepsister as a mercenary instead of learning to solve her own problems. But such moments of doubt were always superseded by Rachel's sense of duty. Sometimes she won the battles and sometimes she lost, but she had never walked away from any of them.

Rachel Wilder was about to fight another battle.

She saw the house when she came around a final bend in the narrow, mountain road. It had to be the right place. It certainly fit the bizarre description she'd received from the attendant at the filling station a few miles back.

"You can't miss the place," the man had assured her cheerfully. "It's called Snowball's Chance. Built by an old miner named Chance, one of the few who actually struck it rich here back in the 1800s. The Chance family has owned it ever since, but they haven't lived here much. Just on and off, you know? Place has been vacant for years now. No one's taken care of it, and the place is kind of falling apart. When I was a kid, me and some friends used to pretend it was haunted. It's real isolated and looks like something out of a nightmare. I remember one Halloween when we—" The attendant broke off and grinned. "Never mind. We were just kids trying to scare ourselves, and we did."

"Can you give me directions?"

"Sure. Stands all alone at the end of a narrow, little road. You'll have to pay attention to find the turnoff. It's not marked. The house is a couple of stories tall with weird little towers, steep roofs and funny-shaped windows. It's got a big, old porch that wraps around the whole thing on the first level and a bunch of little bal-

conies, or whatever you call them, around the second
story. Some of the upper balconies looked like they
were sagging last time I was up there. Probably not too
safe. As I said, no one's bothered to do any repairs in
years. Leastways, not till this guy moved in a few weeks
ago. Heard he's a Chance. Must have inherited the
place and decided to try doing something with it.
Doesn't hardly seem worth the time and money. If I
were him, I'd put it on the market."

Rachel nodded noncommittally, jotted down the directions and thanked the man. Three wrong turns later
she had finally found the narrow track that wound up
the hillside to Snowball's Chance.

As she entered the unpaved drive in front of the
house, she realized what the service station attendant
had meant when he said the place looked like something out of a nightmare. It was a conglomeration of
everything that was overblown, outrageous and bizarre in late-nineteenth-century architecture. The miner
might have been rich enough to indulge his tastes, but
his tastes had clearly been bad, at least by twentieth-
century standards.

The structure stood alone on a hill surrounded by
towering trees. It was the only house for miles as far as
she could tell. When she rolled down the car window
the merest whisper of an early fall wind in the treetops
reinforced the impression of loneliness and isolation.
Unconsciously Rachel shivered.

She slowed the Toyota as she approached the house.
There was another car in the drive, a dusty Chevy, but

no sign of anyone. She switched off the ignition and for a long moment sat behind the wheel of her car, staring at the bizarre house and wondering what she was going to do now that she'd finally tracked Abraham Chance to his lair. It had taken a fair amount of detective work on her part to get this far.

She had taken her vacation leave from work in order to pursue and corner her quarry, but now that he was almost within reach, she wasn't quite sure what she was going to do next.

It wasn't like Rachel to be so ambivalent and uncertain. She was thirty years old, and she had more than her share of self-confidence. She had worked hard to get where she was. In her position as a sophisticated corporate planning analyst in a San Francisco manufacturing firm, she was valued for her efficiency and skill. Rachel Wilder always got the job done, or so her boss had noted on her last merit-raise evaluation.

But Rachel Wilder had never tried her hand at vengeance, nor had she ever tackled a man such as Abraham Chance.

Setting her teeth, she reminded herself she had never backed down from a challenge in her life. She wasn't going to start now. Someone needed to show this man they called Chance that he couldn't wreck the lives of others with impunity.

Rachel saw no one around as she opened the door of the Toyota. She got out of her car slowly, still trying to decide how to handle the coming scene.

During the long drive from San Francisco she had considered everything from threatening a lawsuit to taking her story to a reporter. Unfortunately, none of her limited alternatives had offered much hope of satisfaction, and most of them would only have served to further humiliate her sister, who had already been hurt enough by Abraham Chance.

Rachel closed the car door and stood with her arms folded against the bite of the cool breeze. The neat curve of her golden brown hair, which normally followed the line of her chin, became ruffled in the wind. There were clouds gathering overhead. It looked as if there would be rain tonight. She would have to get back down this hill to a motel before the storm hit. The old, unpaved road that led to Snowball's Chance probably became a river of mud when it rained.

She didn't see or hear the man who came around one corner of the porch roof until he spoke. He stood looking down at her from his high perch, his feet braced slightly apart. He had a hammer in one hand and a length of wood in the other. It was obvious he'd been doing repairs. His voice was gravel and ice on the wind, full of impatience, annoyance and, just perhaps, an element of surprise.

"It's about time you got here," Abraham Chance called down to her. "I had just about given up on that agency. I hope you're not going to turn out to be a nervous, high-strung wimp like the last housekeeper they sent. I haven't got time to cater to dithering, cowering females. I need someone who can do a day's work."

Rachel's head came up with a snap as she caught sight of the man on the porch roof. It was Abraham Chance. It had to be him. Even without her stepsister's emotional and erratic description, Rachel would have guessed his identity. Grim, stark, unhandsome features, a lean, hard body and eyes the color of smoke. He was in his mid-thirties, but something about his face made him appear older. Perhaps it was the utter lack of softness. Chance looked as ruthless and fierce as Gail had claimed he was. But his greeting had disconcerted her.

"You know who I am, Mr. Chance?" she asked in a tone as frigid as she could make it.

His forbidding expression turned slightly more intimidating, if that was possible. "You'd better be from that domestic service agency in Sacramento."

Without waiting for an answer, he crouched at the edge of the porch roof and vaulted lightly over the side. He balanced for an instant on the railing and then jumped easily to the ground and strode purposefully toward her. "I put in an order for another housekeeper, but I got the impression they might not be able to convince anyone else to come. When Mrs. Vinson stormed out of here a couple of days ago, she vowed she'd spread the word about my lack of qualifications as an employer. Mrs. Vinson had the inner fortitude of a mouse. No guts, no backbone, no sense. On top of everything else, she whined a lot. I told the agency I only needed someone for a month, but you'd think she'd been sentenced to Siberia. All I had to do was look at her, and she had an anxiety attack. I hope you're not from the same mold."

Rachel held her breath, mentally adjusting to this unexpected turn of events. He assumed she was a professional housekeeper. Someone he had ordered up from an agency the same way he would order a shirt out of a catalog.

"I seemed to have missed getting the word from Mrs. Vinson," Rachel said slowly. "Just what qualifications are you lacking as an employer, Mr. Chance?"

He scowled as he came to a halt in front of her. Up close he was unexpectedly intimidating. He was wearing only a pair of dusty jeans and scuffed boots. The jeans rode low on his hips, emphasizing a lean, flat waist. He was bare from the waist up, and there were rivulets of sweat streaking his broad shoulders in spite of the brisk breeze. The dampness trickled down through the crisp, curling hair that covered his chest.

It was obvious he'd been engaged in some heavy manual labor on the porch roof when Rachel had arrived. The hand wrapped around the handle of the hammer looked strong and callused. His arms were contoured with sinewy muscle. There was nothing beefy or overdeveloped about him, but there was a definite sense of male strength. Rachel had to stifle an instinctive desire to take a step back. She wasn't accustomed to dealing with naked male power. In her world such power usually came clad in three-piece suits.

"Mrs. Vinson," he said dryly, "apparently left here with the impression that I am rude, demanding, arrogant, impatient and generally difficult." Smoky eyes challenged Rachel.

"And are you all of those things, Mr. Chance?" she asked quietly.

"Probably. Are you going to stick around long enough to find out, or are you going to turn tail and run back down this mountain before the rain hits?"

"I think," Rachel said, making up her mind in a split second, "that I'll stick around and find out if Mrs. Vinson's analysis is correct." Good grief, what was she doing, Rachel wondered wildly. This was insane. Crazy. Dangerous.

But she couldn't stop herself from recklessly reaching out to take the poison apple he was offering. He was virtually inviting her into his home. Once there she would be able to learn a great deal about him, and such knowledge would give her power. The tantalizing opportunity couldn't be ignored, not by a woman whose heart was burning with outrage.

Chance studied her deliberately for a long moment. "All right," he said at last, "we'll give it a try. I'm not expecting you to last any longer than Mrs. Vinson did, but maybe I can get some work out of you before you leave."

"I always give an honest day's work for a day's pay," she assured him blandly.

His eyes roved her slender figure. "You don't look too strong. The kind of cleaning this place needs requires a fair amount of muscle."

"I assure you, I'm stronger than I look."

He still appeared skeptical. "Yeah, well, we'll see what happens. You can start by not calling me mister. People usually call me Chance."

"What about those who don't call you Chance?"

His brows lifted sardonically. "You'd be amazed at how creative some folks can be when it comes to thinking up names for me."

"I'll bet," Rachel murmured. She could think of a few herself.

"Where's your luggage?"

"In the trunk." Car keys jangled in her nervous hand as she went to open the back of the Toyota. This had to be the craziest thing she'd ever done in her life.

He strode toward the car and stood looking down at the overnight case in the trunk. "Is that all you brought? You really aren't planning to stay very long, are you?"

Rachel had expected only to be away from San Francisco overnight, but she decided not to mention that. "I thought I'd see how things worked out on the job before picking up some suitable work clothes. You don't need wool suits and silk blouses for this kind of work, Mr., er, Chance. A pair of jeans and an old shirt are all that's required. I've got one set in here." She patted the overnight case. "I'll get more if I need them."

"Do you always dress like this when you arrive on a job?" Chance demanded, eyeing her crisp, heather-colored wool slacks, cream silk shirt and snug-fitting vest. His gaze dropped lower, taking in the expensive loafers she was wearing.

Uncomfortably aware that the slacks, shirt, vest and shoes were not the sort of things one expected to find a housekeeper wearing, Rachel decided to take the offensive. This man was a trained investigator, according to her stepsister, the ruthless, predatory agent of Dixon Security Inc. He would not be easily fooled.

"Your image of professional housekeepers is as out-of-date as your house, Chance," Rachel said. She lifted the overnight bag out of the trunk. "Those of us who are making a career out of the housekeeping business these days are trying to update the old-fashioned, dowdy impression. Now if you'll kindly show me where I'll be staying?"

He blinked owlishly. "Do you have a name?"

"Rachel Wilder." He wouldn't make any connections, she thought. Her stepsister's last name was Vaughan.

"All right, Rachel. I'll show you to your room. Then I'll show you the kitchen. It's almost time for dinner. During dinner I'll give you a rundown on what I want you to do while you're working here." Without another word he started toward the house.

Rachel followed, drawing a deep, steadying breath while she tried to settle her nerves and calm her racing pulse. She could feel the adrenaline shooting through her system, leaving her first hot and then cold. This was stupid. She couldn't hope to carry off the deception for very long. Abraham Chance would be enraged when he realized what was happening.

But so what?

It would serve him right, Rachel thought angrily. In the meantime she might learn something useful about him, something that would allow her to pay him back for what he'd done to her sister. If nothing else, it would infuriate and possibly humiliate him to learn he'd been fool enough to take the enemy into his home. It wasn't much in the way of revenge, but it would be better than just yelling at him.

As she followed him into the dank and dusty hallway, Rachel surreptitiously studied her victim. He wasn't quite as tall or as large as she'd expected. But, then, she had to make allowances for Gail's understandably biased impressions. Abraham Chance had no doubt seemed huge and ferocious the day he'd brought Gail's world tumbling down around her ears. Any man who first seduced a woman and then turned on her, accusing her of theft, publicly humiliating her and topping it off by causing her to lose her job, probably seemed much bigger and taller than he actually was.

Nevertheless, Rachel decided, the impression of physical strength that emanated from the man was undeniable.

His stride was long, easy and coordinated. His hair was nearly black. Perhaps he normally kept it cut quite short, but it seemed to have gotten a bit long lately, as if he hadn't wanted to spare the time for a haircut. The combination of smoky eyes and dark hair would have been a handsome one in some men, but in this man the overall impression was of forbidding darkness.

Rachel switched her attention to her surroundings and decided Abraham Chance's house was every bit as forbidding as he was. Paint was peeling from the walls, the windows were dingy with years of grime and the wooden floors were scuffed and scarred. Old drapes sagged from their rods, the furniture looked as if it belonged in a yard sale and the glass lighting fixtures were so dark with dust and dead insects that very little light escaped to illuminate the rooms.

Rachel shuddered as she started up the uncarpeted stairs behind her new employer. She was a fool, she told herself once more. If she had any sense she would run while she still could. But the lure of revenge was too strong to resist.

Outside, the first scattered drops of rain began to fall, harbingers of the storm that was to follow.

Chance was aware of an unexpectedly awkward sensation as he led his new housekeeper down the hall to the room that had been so recently vacated by Mrs. Vinson. It took him a while to recognize the uneasy feeling and, when he finally identified it as embarrassment, he was annoyed with himself.

It was dumb, he realized ruefully, but he was actually embarrassed to have Rachel Wilder see the cracked and peeling paint on the walls, the scarred hardwood floors and the precariously hanging chandelier at the top of the stairs. One of these days it was going to collapse. Rachel Wilder looked like the kind of woman who would complain long and loudly if it happened to fall on her toe. She'd probably sue him to hell and back. The woman looked like the feisty type. Something within him stirred at the thought. He decided he liked the feisty type. It made a nice change from the weak, melodramatic, whining females he always seemed to encounter.

Abraham Chance had no patience with fools and whining females, and he made no pretense about it.

This Rachel Wilder looked as though she might be a pleasant change. He had to remind himself that she wasn't exactly a guest in this house. She was a housekeeper, and she was here to help him put Snowball's Chance back together.

But he sensed it was going to be tough to keep that in mind. When he'd first seen her standing beside her car in her polished loafers, expensive slacks and fashionable shirt, he'd wondered if she was a tourist who had accidentally wandered off the main road and stopped for directions. Rachel Wilder just did not look like a housekeeper. She looked like a woman who was accustomed to giving orders, not taking them.

Maybe she was right. Perhaps he did have a few preconceived images of housekeepers. Mrs. Vinson had lived up to every one of them. Rachel did not.

She was too slender, for one thing, too delicately put together. He wondered critically how she was going to find the strength to clean the windows of the two-story house. What fullness there was to her figure was definitely not in her shoulder and arm muscles. As far as he could tell it was around her hips. She had a very nicely rounded rear, he decided. It was difficult to gauge the size and shape of her breasts beneath the vest, but Chance had the impression she was built on the small side in that department.

Her hair didn't fit his image of a housekeeper's bob, either. The sort of style Rachel Wilder wore came out of a salon, not a beauty shop. He was intrigued by the color of that hair, a rich, golden brown that caught the light and gleamed. She wore it in a simple style, parted in the center and gently curved in a line that followed her chin on either side. Chance wondered what it would feel like to put his fingers beneath that neat curve of hair and find the soft, sensitive place at the nape of her neck. He had a hunch he'd need stitches in his hand if he tried such a maneuver without her permission. The image made him grin inwardly.

Unfortunately, the thought of Miss Wilder's undoubted temper only caused him to speculate about her capacity for other kinds of passion. She had eyes that would glow with her mood, Chance decided. Blue-green gems fringed with long, soft lashes.

The lines of her face were subtle, not striking or riveting but oddly alluring. There was a definite hint of stubbornness in the firm chin and the strong line of her nose. She had nice bones beneath her eyes. They gave her a touch of regalness that he found as interesting as it was challenging. The physical awareness that had stirred to life deep within him when he'd first seen Rachel was now coming to full alertness.

Chance stifled a groan as he threw open the door of a bedroom. That was all he needed. The idea of seducing his live-in housekeeper was as stupid as it was ridiculous. He needed some real work done around this place. He definitely did not need a lover. Besides, Miss Wilder didn't look as though she would be at all attracted to the notion of tending to his physical needs at night, after she'd put in a full day's work tending to this dilapidated house.

"Sorry," he muttered, watching her survey the shabby bedroom with its decayed wallpaper and old, abused furniture. "This is the best there is at the moment. The other bedrooms are in much worse shape. The place needs a lot of work, as you can see."

"Have you considered simply bulldozing it down and starting over?" Rachel moved into the room with fastidious care. She walked as a ballerina would through a dirty alley, careful not to touch anything.

Chance was suddenly irritated by her attitude. "Admittedly this isn't the Ritz but, then, you're a housekeeper, not visiting royalty. You must have known what you were getting into when you accepted the position."

"The agency's description of the place didn't do it justice." There was a note of dry amusement in the comment.

"Snowball's Chance is basically sound," Chance informed her proudly. "The wood is solid, and the foundation's fine. My great-great-grandfather built this place to last. The wiring is a little outdated, but I'm taking care of that. The appliances downstairs are old, but they still work." He hesitated, remembering the trouble he'd had with the stove that morning when he'd put the kettle on for coffee. "Sort of," he amended.

"That's wonderful news," Rachel assured him coolly as she strolled cautiously around the small room. "What about the plumbing?"

He watched her through narrow eyes. "What about it?"

She smiled a little too brilliantly. "I assume it is the, uh, indoor version?"

Chance planted his hands on his hips, thoroughly annoyed now. "Yes, as a matter of fact, it is. Right down the hall. We'll have to share. There's a second bathroom at the other end of the hall, but I haven't got it in working order yet."

"We're going to have to share a bathroom?"

"It's a bathroom, not a bedroom, Miss Wilder," Chance retorted. "I'm sure we'll manage to stay out of each other's way."

"I'm sure we will." She swung around to face the window as if something outside had caught her attention, but Chance was certain he'd seen a trace of red on her cheeks. Well, it served her right. He hadn't meant to embarrass her, but the lady had asked for it. Next she would probably be asking which number to dial for room service.

"Look, Miss Wilder, I think we'd better get a few things clear between us," Chance began aggressively. "I need some real work done around here. I do not need a delicate, fussy little prima donna who's going to complain about the working conditions every time she turns around. If you don't think you can handle the job, just say so."

She glanced back at him over her shoulder, and Chance saw the flare of determination in her eyes. "Don't worry, Chance, I'm staying, regardless of the conditions. Now if you'll excuse me, I'd like to change and get ready to cook dinner. I assume there is some food in the house?"

"I bought some things yesterday," he said slowly, wondering at the forcefulness in her tone. "Check the refrigerator and the cupboards. I'm not very particular about what I eat so long as it isn't burned to a crisp."

"I'll remember that. The sooner you leave, the sooner I can get started on your dinner." She stood waiting for him to back out of the room as if, instead of her new employer, he were the bellhop who had just carried up her luggage.

Chance hesitated a long moment, aware of an abrupt, almost overpowering desire to do something that would shatter the chilly feminine arrogance in her eyes. Then common sense reasserted itself. The fact was, he needed her. After Mrs. Vinson had stormed out, he had worried that he wouldn't be able to find anyone to stick around long enough to get the inside of

Snowball's Chance in shape. If he had any brains he wouldn't drive off Rachel Wilder.

"I'll see you downstairs, Rachel," he said, and forced himself to walk out of the dingy room.

THE BREEZE OUTSIDE turned into a full-scale, howling wind as the storm struck later that night. Lightning flashed in the darkness, and the rain pelted with insistent force against the windows of Chance's bedroom.

Chance lay in bed, his arms folded behind his head, the sheet and blankets bunched carelessly at his waist. The room was getting cold and would get a lot colder before morning, but he wasn't thinking of that. His mind drifted back over the rich, hearty stew Rachel had managed to put together from the odds and ends she'd found in the kitchen. There had been a thick slice of rye bread and a dollop of sour cream to accompany the filling concoction. He wondered how she'd wrung so much flavor out of the minimal condiments and spices he'd stocked.

For an expensively dressed prima donna who looked as though she'd turn up her nose at anything that wasn't made with truffles or Brie cheese, she had acquitted herself well in the kitchen.

What was even more important, she seemed to understand that a man who had been doing hard manual labor all day appreciated his glass of Scotch before dinner. She had found the bottle in the kitchen cupboard and had had a drink waiting for him when he'd come downstairs after showering. He'd been mildly surprised but had said nothing when she'd joined him in the old-fashioned parlor, in front of the fire, with a glass of her own. She had appeared to need the drink more than he had. It made him curious.

But Chance had also discovered it was rather pleasant to share a predinner Scotch with Rachel. He found himself hoping the whole thing might become a nice little ritual, one he could look forward to at the end of the day.

He'd used the opportunity to outline his requirements in a housekeeper. Chance had told himself that with a woman like this, he needed to make certain she understood who was the boss right from the start.

"I've got my hands full with repairs on the outside of the house. I want to get that kind of thing taken care of before winter hits. I want you to get the inside in decent shape. The closets and cupboards are full of old junk that needs to be sorted out. Discard the unusable stuff. I'll haul it to the dump or give it to charity. Also the windows need cleaning."

"Along with everything else," she had concluded dryly, glancing around the parlor in cool disdain.

Chance had forgiven her the rude comment after he'd tasted her stew.

If a man was prone to self-delusion he could almost convince himself that Miss Wilder really was a trained cook and, therefore, just perhaps, a full-fledged housekeeper.

But Chance wasn't inclined to delude himself. He had spent too many years making a career out of uncovering illusions, fraud and other assorted games. He knew instinctively when something wasn't right.

And there was something very wrong about the concept of Miss Wilder as a professional housekeeper.

He remembered the grim determination in her gaze that afternoon when she'd informed him she would be staying in spite of shared plumbing, bad wiring and hard work.

There was not a doubt in Chance's mind that Rachel Wilder would have turned her Toyota around and headed right back down the hill the instant she caught sight of Snowball's Chance—if she'd had any choice in the matter. For some reason she had elected to stay.

There were a limited number of reasons why a woman might choose to work as a housekeeper in a remote location if housekeeping weren't her usual profession.

The most logical reason was that Rachel was hiding from something or someone.

Chance examined that possibility from a variety of angles. If she was hiding from a man, he must be dangerous. It would take a great deal to drive Rachel Wilder into hiding from a mere male.

It was equally possible she was hiding from an unpleasant situation. Perhaps she'd gotten involved in a nasty little love triangle and was running from the inevitable scene that would ensue.

Chance grimaced. He didn't like that prospect. For some reason he didn't want to think of Rachel involved in a passionate triangle. Nor did he think it very likely. She was too fastidious, too proud to get into that kind of mess.

Chance made himself go on to another possibility. It was conceivable she was running from something illegal. Not very probable, because again he didn't think she was the type, but it was just barely conceivable. He'd worked for Dixon Security long enough to know you couldn't always tell a book by its cover. And women were notoriously hard to read. The sweetest, most rosy-cheeked little accounting clerks could turn out to be the most efficient embezzlers.

There were a variety of reasons why a woman might choose to hide. From his experience, Chance knew most of them. But he was startled to discover that when he tried to analyze those reasons in regard to Rachel Wilder, it wasn't just his curiosity that was aroused. He wound up feeling violently protective.

He sighed and reached for the blankets. It was oddly pleasant to think of the spirited Miss Wilder sleeping just down the hall. He was experiencing a physical anticipation and awareness that elicited a vague, sweet ache somewhere in the region below his waist.

Tomorrow he would check with the domestic service agency just to make certain his guess was accurate. If it confirmed his deduction that she wasn't a professional housekeeper, he was going to have an interesting problem.

But, then, Miss Wilder was an interesting package. Chance promised himself he would unwrap her slowly and carefully. There was no rush.

2

RACHEL SPENT a restless night. She was disturbed by both the storm and her incredibly bold move in choosing to masquerade as Abraham Chance's housekeeper. Her own daring almost took her breath away. She had stayed awake a long time, thinking about it and wondering if she'd done the right thing. By dawn she was consoling herself with the thought that the traumatic, vicious deception Chance had perpetrated on her stepsister left no room for second thoughts or poor-spirited doubts when it came to revenge. This was her big chance, Rachel told herself, and then winced at the pun. . . .

By dawn the storm had abated, leaving behind a clear sky and a forest of dripping trees. Unfortunately, Rachel's uneasiness hadn't settled down or vanished along with the rain.

But she felt committed now to seizing the opportunity. It was a cinch she would never have another opportunity to get this close to the enemy. She must learn what she could and then have the guts to use whatever it was she learned.

Thrusting aside the bedclothes, she shrugged into her lightweight travel robe and hurried down the cold hall to the even colder bathroom. If she was lucky she could be in and out before her employer arose.

The shower was an old-fashioned metal ring affair that probably dated from the 1930s. Rachel eyed it with misgivings, but when she turned on the tap, water immediately pumped through the pipes.

Cold water.

"Give me strength," Rachel muttered.

She waited a few more minutes. The water didn't change temperature. It was as cold as when she'd first turned it on. She would probably freeze into a nude popsicle the minute she stepped into the tub, but she simply couldn't stand the thought of starting the day without a shower.

Gritting her teeth, she stepped under the cold spray. The shock of the icy water made her gasp. Two and a half minutes later she exited the tub, certain she had just completed the shortest shower on record. Chance would hear about this at breakfast, she vowed as she tugged on her designer jeans and a long-sleeved sweater she'd brought along for the drive back to San Francisco.

When he sauntered downstairs fifteen minutes behind her, she had hot oatmeal, toast and coffee waiting. He was dressed much as he had been yesterday, in jeans and low boots, but at least he'd had the good manners to wear a flannel shirt down to breakfast. His hair was still damp from what must have been an exceedingly cold shower. Inhaling the coffee aroma appreciatively, Chance nodded a friendly good-morning and sank into the nearest chair.

"Glad to see you're an early riser. The coffee smells good." He reached for the coffeepot, oblivious to the way Rachel was standing, her feet slightly apart, her hands balled into small fists on her hips. "I'm starving. Hope you slept okay last night. That storm was a loud one, wasn't it?"

"The storm," she said bluntly, "was not my main problem."

He paused with the cup halfway to his mouth. He appeared far more interested in her comment than Rachel would have expected under the circumstances. His gray eyes were intent and serious and surprisingly gentle. "What is your main problem, Rachel?" The gravel and ice of his voice produced a soft rumble.

She frowned, not understanding his odd, coaxing tone. "You should know. You took a shower right after I did. The water was like ice."

"Oh, that." He shrugged, the intent interest in his eyes vanishing. "The water heater just needs a little fine-tuning, that's all. I'll take care of it after breakfast. Why don't you sit down and eat? Your coffee's getting cold."

"Chance, I would like to make it perfectly clear that I am not accustomed to ice-water showers. The situation will have to be remedied. Are you going to be able to get the hot water heater functioning properly on a regular basis?" Unconsciously she used the same tone of voice she would have used on a slow-working, obstinate clerk or secretary. She sat down across from him and reached for the chipped bowl of brown sugar in the center of the old, wobbly kitchen table.

Chance eyed her for a moment, his gaze unreadable. "Are you threatening to leave unless I can provide hot water?"

"I do not consider hot water a luxury. I consider it a necessity."

He nodded, looking resigned. "You would. I knew the minute I saw you that you were going to be a demanding little thing."

"I am not a little thing," she retorted. "Furthermore, I do not consider myself demanding. I am merely asking for a minimum of amenities. I hardly think it's too much to request decent plumbing in one's place of employment. There are certain federal and state requirements that make it mandatory, in fact. Also, I would like to point out—"

The loud, shrilling ring of a telephone interrupted her. Chance winced, although he looked suspiciously relieved at the interruption. "You get it. Answering phones should be a housekeeper's job. Tell whoever it is that the answer is no."

Rachel stared at him. "But you don't even know who's calling."

"The possibilities are limited, but I prefer to avoid all of them." The phone rang again. "The phone is in the hall," he added encouragingly. "Just pick it up and say 'no.'"

Irritated, Rachel jumped to her feet and went into the hall. The phone, an old-fashioned plain black instrument, shrilled again. She yanked the receiver off the cradle.

"Hello?"

"Let me speak to Chance." The voice on the other end was gruff, imperious and male. "Now."

Rachel cleared her throat. "I'm afraid Mr. Chance cannot come to the phone right now," she said in her coolest professional tone.

There was a startled pause on the other end of the line. And then the gruff voice demanded, "Who is this?"

"His housekeeper."

"His housekeeper! What the hell's he doing up there? Playing gentleman farmer? Has he got an upstairs maid and a butler now, too? Listen, lady, Chance works for me. Get him on the line and do it immediately."

Rachel's fingers tightened around the phone, and her voice became infinitely chillier. "May I say who is calling, please?"

"Tell him it's Dixon, for crying out loud!"

Dixon. She was speaking to the head of Dixon Security, the company that had been hired to investigate the thefts at the firm where her sister had worked. "I'm sorry, Mr. Dixon, I've been instructed to tell all callers that Mr. Chance is unavailable."

"Bull. You tell Chance if he doesn't get on the line now he's not going to have a job."

Rachel considered her options. She couldn't believe Chance had known who was calling when he instructed her to say no to everyone. Apparently he was in trouble with his boss. Surely he would want to take this call. She wondered how much damage she would do to his career if she simply followed orders.

"The answer is no, Mr. Dixon. Goodbye." She hung up the phone before the man on the other end had stopped sputtering. She stood for a moment staring at the receiver, wondering what she'd just done and then, slowly, her nerves tingling, she walked back into the kitchen.

"Who was it?" Chance asked without much interest. He was halfway through his cereal. The pile of toast at his elbow had almost disappeared.

"A man named Dixon. He said he was your boss," Rachel murmured very sweetly. "He asked to speak to you, and I did as you instructed. I told him no." She waited for the explosion. When it didn't take place she didn't know whether to be relieved or disappointed.

"Good. Maybe that will keep him off my back for a while." Chance poured himself another cup of coffee.

Rachel cleared her throat. "*Is* he your boss?" she asked carefully.

"Former boss. I quit a couple of weeks ago."

"I see." She didn't know what to say to that. Apparently she hadn't done his career much damage by hanging up. "Uh, why did you quit?"

"Dixon and I had a disagreement about the handling of my last assignment," Chance said in clipped tones. "There were some questions left that I thought should have been answered. I wanted to finish the investigation, but the client was satisfied with the results at that point and wanted to cut off further inquiries. It wasn't the first such disagreement Dixon and I have had over the years, but I decided it would definitely be the last. I told him to go to hell, and he gave me roughly the same instructions. But I didn't follow orders. I came up here instead."

"Why is he calling you if he fired you?"

Chance lifted one shoulder in negligent dismissal. "Weren't you listening? He didn't fire me. I quit. And who knows why he's calling? Probably because he wants me to go back to work for him."

"And you don't want to?"

"Nope. I've been looking for a good excuse to quit, and this is it."

This was getting complicated, Rachel thought. But she decided to persevere. She had to know what was going on if she was going to make any realistic plans for revenge. Obviously she would have to drop the possibility of getting Chance into trouble with his boss. Abraham Chance was already in trouble with his boss and didn't much care.

"Are you going to work for someone else?" Rachel asked cautiously.

He glanced up from his oatmeal, obviously surprised by her interest in the subject. Rachel wondered if she'd moved too fast.

"I'm thinking of starting my own company," he said after a slight pause.

"A security firm like Dixon's? One that specializes in corporate security work?" Rachel asked too quickly.

"How did you know I was in that kind of work?"

She bit her lip and picked up her spoon. This sort of thing could get tricky. "Oh, something your boss said on the phone. I believe he identified himself as head of a company called Dixon Security."

"Did he?"

Rachel coughed delicately. "Would you like some more toast?"

"Sure."

She got up quickly and went to the counter to shove two more slices of bread into the old toaster. "At least this appliance works," she said with unwarranted enthusiasm.

"Yes, it does," he said. There was almost no inflection in his voice.

When she glanced back at him, she saw that he was watching her with an unreadable expression. "So," she forced herself to go on brightly, "I'm just to say no to anyone else who calls?"

"That's right."

"Are you expecting a lot of calls?"

"I'm expecting to be pestered by certain people. I shall rely on you to protect my privacy. Isn't that part of a good housekeeper's job?"

She wasn't quite sure what to say to that. "Of course," she finally mumbled, turning back to the toaster.

"This arrangement can work both ways, you know," he finally said, his voice softening unexpectedly. That particular tone sounded quite rusty, as if he wasn't accustomed to trying to sound gentle and unthreatening.

Rachel swung around, startled. "What do you mean?"

His mouth curved slightly, and there was an oddly reassuring, very confident smile in his eyes. "I'm willing to protect your privacy in exchange for your guarding mine."

"I don't understand."

"Don't you?" He shrugged again and picked up his coffee. "Well, we'll give it time. Remind me before I go outside this morning to give you a few warnings about the washing machine. It's temperamental."

"Somehow that doesn't come as a surprise." Relieved to have the subject changed, Rachel pursued another topic. "What are you planning to do with this house, Chance? Fix it up and sell it?"

"Fix it up and *keep* it. I told you this place was built by my great-great-grandfather. He was a little eccentric, but after he struck it rich in the gold fields hereabouts he became a rich eccentric."

"That does make a difference."

"You bet. He poured a lot of money into this place and named it Snowball's Chance, which was what everyone said his odds were of getting rich in California. He married a San Francisco lady and brought her here to live. Unfortunately, my great-great-grandmother was not as fond of Snowball's Chance as her husband was. She began complaining about the lack of the kind of social life she'd enjoyed in San Francisco. She tried to persuade her husband to move back to the city."

"And he refused to listen to her pleas?" Rachel hazarded dryly.

"How did you know?"

"I have a feeling excessive stubbornness and arrogance run in the male side of your family."

Chance smiled wickedly. "I can understand great-great-grandfather's feelings on the subject. Whining, complaining women are irritating as hell."

"I can assure you that whining, complaining men are no more pleasant," Rachel snapped. "I've met plenty of both."

Chance considered that carefully and then nodded in agreement. "You're right. But for some reason I always seem to run into the female variety. I could tell you stories about my last secretary that would make you shudder. She was always moaning about something or other. Always had an excuse for not getting her work done. Then there's my Aunt Agatha. According to her, she's been at death's door for the past twenty years. A total hypochondriac. And my sister—"

"We were discussing your great-great-grandfather."

"Yeah. Well, Great-great-grandfather finally lost his patience and told his wife to shut up and choose between him and the bright lights of San Francisco. He wasn't about to leave Snowball's Chance. This place meant a lot to him. It was the symbol of everything he'd been looking for when he came West. It was the visible evidence of his success and good luck."

"What happened to your great-great-grandmother?"

Chance's smile broadened into a grin. "She suddenly found herself pregnant, and that made her eminently reasonable. She stopped having tantrums and settled down to being a wife and a mother."

"In this house?" Rachel asked skeptically.

"Sure. This was the house her husband chose to provide. She decided to make it into a home."

Rachel nodded soberly. "Women in those days didn't have many options, especially if they got pregnant."

"Don't look so sad for Great-great-grandmother. From all accounts she was a happy woman once she'd ceased trying to manipulate her husband."

"Uh-huh. So your ancestor gave your great-great-grandmother an ultimatum and managed to bully her into staying here. What happened to the next couple of generations?" She deftly caught the toast as it leaped out of the toaster.

Chance scowled at her summary of the situation. "The next generation of Chances was born and raised here, too. But by Dad's generation things had changed."

"You mean women had gotten a little more assertive?"

"I guess. All I know is that my father never came back here to live after he left to go into the army. When he got out he married and stayed in the San Francisco Bay area. That's where I was born and raised. But Dad never got around to selling this place. He tried renting it out a couple of times, and once in a while we came here for vacation in the summer, but that was about it."

"But you loved it here, right?"

Chance smiled again. "Right. I liked the idea that it had been in the family since Great-great-grandfather's day. Something about the historical connection appeals to me, I suppose. Funny, because I am definitely not the sentimental type."

"I believe you," Rachel said coolly. If there was any real sentimentality in this man, it was buried under an awful lot of steel.

He ignored her interruption. "For me the house is a link of some kind. My mother and sister have no interest in the place, though. It's been sitting empty for years. My work has required a lot of traveling. I haven't had a really permanent address since I went off to college. Then, a year ago, Dad died."

"I'm sorry," Rachel said awkwardly. She resented the fact that she felt any sympathy at all for this man. He certainly didn't deserve it.

"He'd had a long, reasonably happy life," Chance said quietly. "How much more can a man ask? But he did manage to put a monkey wrench into my life before he departed."

"How's that?"

"He didn't leave me anything but this house. He thought money was bad for a man's sense of ambition. That was fine with me. I've always taken care of myself, and the house was the only thing I wanted, anyway. But he did leave a couple of sizable trust funds for my mother and sister. Unfortunately, I got saddled with the job of administering the funds. Beth doesn't mind."

"Which one's Beth?"

"My mother. I've called her Beth for years. She hates dealing with numbers, but Mindy, my sister, has other opinions. By the terms of the will, I can't get out of the responsibility of handling her money until she marries or until she turns thirty, whichever comes first. Knowing Mindy, marriage will definitely come first."

"That should let you off the hook."

"Not exactly," Chance said with a groan. "I'm supposed to approve of the marriage before I sign over the papers."

"I think I see the problem."

"Problems, plural. Mindy is barely twenty years old, and already she's been madly in love at least a half dozen times. She's constantly nagging me about not having control of her own money. Drives me bats."

Rachel sat down slowly and reached for her coffee cup. "I have a younger sister, too. Having one can be quite a responsibility."

He grinned wryly. "You're telling me. Mindy is a genuine pain in the neck at times. It's probably because she was born late in my parents' lives and was consequently severely spoiled."

"But you continue to do your duty by her?"

"I'm stuck with it."

Rachel nodded, reluctantly understanding the situation and wishing very much that she did not. Never in a million years would it have occurred to her that Chance might be in the same situation, having to protect a younger sister, as she herself was. Rachel found it vastly annoying to discover she had something in common with Abraham Chance. It was easier to keep one's enemy at an impersonal distance—safer, too. It was surely very dangerous to start seeing him in human terms.

"Who else besides your boss is likely to call and annoy you?" Rachel asked crisply as she began to clear the table. "I should be prepared, don't you think?"

"It's possible Mindy or Beth might call. More likely you'll hear from a guy named Braxton."

"Who's he?"

"Some damn-fool free-lance writer. He used to be a newspaper reporter, but now he's on his own. He claims he wants to do an article on me."

Rachel glanced at Chance in surprise. "Why?"

Chance grimaced. "Unfortunately, one of Dixon Security's happy clients sang the firm's praises too loudly at a cocktail party one evening. He mentioned me by name, apparently. Braxton was there and picked up on the idea of doing an article on the new corporate security business. He says he wants to profile someone in the field, and he's chosen me."

Rachel's fingers trembled a little as she picked up a tattered dishrag. "That's very interesting. You don't want to be profiled?"

"Hell, no. Braxton's a sleazy pest. I figure if I ignore him long enough he'll give up and go away. I've got better things to do with my time than feed him a story." Chance got to his feet. "So get rid of him if he calls. I'd better go have a look at that hot water tank." He strode toward the door and then paused. "After I deal with the hot water problem I'm going to be in the old coach house out back. There's a lot of equipment and tools and assorted junk stored out there. I've got to sort through it and decide what to toss. Holler if you need me."

"All right. I'm going to have to make a trip into town in a couple of hours. Your cupboards are bare."

"Get what you need, and I'll reimburse you. Oh, and Rachel?"

She looked around warily, expecting more orders. "Yes?"

"Breakfast was okay. You make a mean cup of coffee. Mrs. Vinson's was terrible."

He went out into the hall, leaving Rachel staring after him. Life was, indeed, getting complicated.

TWO HOURS LATER Chance stood in front of the coach house wiping his hands on a dirty rag as he watched Rachel head for town in her Toyota. He wondered how many professional housekeepers went to work in designer jeans. Not that she didn't look very good in them, he thought.

When the Toyota had disappeared from sight, Chance tossed aside the rag and headed for the house. It was time to make a call and find out if the lady was as mysterious as he was beginning to think she was.

Inside the house, he dialed the number of the domestic service agency that had provided him with Mrs. Vinson.

"I'm very sorry, Mr. Chance, but we simply don't have anyone else to send at the moment," the frosty voice on the other end of the line informed him. "It's unfortunate Mrs. Vinson didn't work out. She was our last available housekeeper. We'll call you if we locate anyone else who might be suitable."

Translated, that meant Mrs. Vinson had already spread the word that Snowball's Chance was not exactly a plum assignment. Women these days could be damn choosy.

Chance replaced the receiver with a thoughtful air. He had his first answer about Miss Rachel Wilder. She definitely was not from the domestic service agency that had sent Mrs. Vinson.

He went back out to the coach house, where he'd been inventorying several years' worth of broken tools, discarded appliances, rusted gardening equipment, auto parts, and the other assorted debris that tended to collect in such places over a period of time. He had been delighted to discover that a great deal of the stuff was still in useful condition.

The coach house was a tall building that had originally been designed to shelter carriages and buggies. It had later been used for automobiles, but there was no room inside these days for a car. The accumulation of junk filled most of the first level; more was piled in the loft overhead. A ladder led up to the loft, and the place was illuminated by a dingy light bulb that hung from a chain attached to the ceiling. The light didn't extend much above the first level. Telling himself that he would have to rig up something better one of these days, Chance went back to work.

There was a treasure trove of useful objects to be inventoried, and Chance was enjoying the process. They didn't make hammers the way they used to, he thought as he examined a rusty specimen. The wooden shaft was broken, but the iron head was still in great condition. He hefted it. Nice balance. One of these days he'd see about replacing the handle. He tossed it into the save pile.

He went on to a tangle of wrenches that had lain for years in an old, rusted-out toolbox. A man could collect wrenches for a lifetime and still not have just the right size he needed in a true plumbing emergency. Chance went through the wrenches one by one and finally opted to keep them all. Better to be safe than sorry.

As yet, there was nothing in the discard pile.

While he sorted through the valuable junk, Chance let his mind play with the mystery surrounding Rachel Wilder.

It was possible she was a personal friend of Mrs. Vinson's who had needed a job. Mrs. Vinson might have quietly passed along the information that work was available if Rachel was really desperate and then told the agency not to bother sending anyone else.

But even if that were the case, it didn't answer many questions. It was obvious that Rachel wasn't a career housekeeper, in spite of her lectures on the subject of professional image. Chance knew a lot about professional images, and he knew where he'd seen Rachel's type in the past.

Young women like her were usually found working their way up through some corporation's management ranks. Or running their own entrepreneurial firms. Or married to successful men and raising successful children. Women with Rachel's image rarely took on jobs as housekeepers in remote locations working under less than ideal conditions.

Okay, Chance thought, so she's not a housekeeper. She might be another free-lance writer like that pesty Braxton. Perhaps she had met Mrs. Vinson, and when the older woman had left, she'd used the opportunity to insinuate herself into the household. A definite possibility.

Chance hefted an old saw, liking the feel of the wooden grip. So what if the blade was missing a few teeth? He decided to keep the tool. A man needed good tools around a house like Snowball's Chance. Old houses required a lot of attention. He put it on the save pile and went back to thinking about Rachel.

The nervy lady free-lancer scenario played well until you considered the wary expression in Rachel's blue-green eyes, Chance decided. She was a woman with something to hide, and he didn't think it was just her desire for a good story. There was too much emotion in that sea-colored gaze. She wanted something more than an article from Snowball's Chance and from him.

He wondered how much more and how far she would go to get it.

Then he smiled grimly to himself. Time was definitely on his side. He was planning to devote most of the fall to Snowball's Chance. When winter arrived he would start making plans for his business future. One thing was for certain: he was not going back to work for Herb Dixon.

In the meantime, it would be interesting to continue unraveling the secrets of Rachel Wilder.

Chance paused once more, lifting an ancient drill out of a cardboard box of metal objects. If he was really lucky he might find some bits around nearby.

He stood gazing down at the drill and realized that he didn't really want to investigate Rachel Wilder as though she were just another assignment. What he really wanted was for Rachel to learn to trust him enough to tell him her secrets.

That would be a very satisfying way, indeed, to spend the next month.

Chance smiled to himself. She was a cautious, wary, prickly little thing. He would have to tread gently if he wanted her to confide in him. He would have to be patient.

There were a number of people in the world who did not consider Abraham Chance the patient sort. They would have been surprised to see the smile on his face.

TWO DAYS LATER Chance stood in the doorway of the coach house and watched Rachel return from another trip to town. This time she'd bought a large load of cleaning supplies. She hadn't dawdled, Chance was pleased to note. He hadn't coaxed any secrets out of her yet, but he was getting his money's worth in terms of housekeeping.

Unfortunately, he found that fact extremely frustrating. He was doing his best to lure her into his confidence, but she seemed totally oblivious to his patient ploys and encouraging hints. This business of being subtle and persuasive was not his normal way of working. He preferred to jump in with both feet and get straight to the heart of the matter. But as he walked across the yard to help carry in sacks of cleaning supplies, he reminded himself that he had to have patience.

When Rachel called him to lunch a bit later he was genuinely appreciative of the solid fare she provided. He realized he was growing accustomed to the good food and the little evening ritual of Scotch in front of the fire. A man could get spoiled.

"I'm going to try a washing this afternoon," she said as he finished the large sandwich she'd made for him. "Maybe you'd better give me another short course on temperamental washing machines."

He nodded agreeably and ran her through the various methods of coaxing the old washer into action. He just wished it was as easy to coax Rachel into confiding.

"Did you send for the rest of your clothes?" he asked conversationally as he watched her dump in the first load of washing. "You didn't bring much with you in that overnight case."

She glanced up, her expression uneasy for an instant. She masked the look quickly. "I picked up a couple of things in town. They'll hold me for a while."

So she wasn't sure yet if she would be staying long enough to warrant sending for her clothes. Either that, or she was afraid the action might tip off someone as to her current location. Chance nodded, deciding not to push her any further on that particular subject.

"There's a line out back where you can hang these things to dry," he said as he started for the door.

"There's no dryer?" she demanded, sounding dismayed.

"Nope. I'll get one before winter sets in, but for now you're going to have to grab what sun you can get."

Her muttered reply was lost amid the churning, clanking noises that the old washing machine was emitting. Chance took the opportunity to escape. Rachel was definitely not accustomed to roughing it, nor did she see anything particularly amusing or adventurous about having to endure the limited conveniences of life here at Snowball's Chance. The fact that she was enduring them at all certainly made a man wonder about her reasons.

But he would say one thing for her. She didn't whine. She definitely stated her opinions on certain subjects, and she wasn't above making demands, but she didn't nag. She said what she thought, but then she went ahead and got the job done, anyway. Chance appreciated that attitude. It was the way he himself went through life.

He whistled tunelessly on the way back to the coach house.

An hour later Chance was jolted to his feet by a woman's scream. The voice was Rachel's, and it was loaded with fury as well as a certain amount of genuine fear. Chance dropped the rusted auto fender he had been studying and raced for the door of the coach house.

It didn't take him long to locate Rachel. She was lying on her back in the empty fish pond, her arms and legs thoroughly tangled in a length of clothesline that had apparently come loose from its moorings overhead. Two of Chance's shirts and a sheet were draped around her.

The pond hadn't been used in years, but there was an inch or two of water in it from last night's rainfall. Just enough to create a nice layer of mud. Rachel was floundering in it.

Chance came to a halt at the edge of the fish pond and stood studying the situation. His new housekeeper looked touchingly vulnerable and surprisingly sweet lying in a web of clothesline.

"Don't just stand there grinning like an idiot," Rachel yelped. "Help me out of here. This is all your fault, anyway. You're the one who hasn't bothered to invest in a decent dryer." She managed to struggle to an upright position. The clothesline and assorted muddy clothes hampered her movements. "Well?" she added challengingly when he didn't move immediately to her rescue. "Aren't you going to help me out of here?"

"There's no rush," Chance said softly as he struggled to control his laughter. "You look kind of interesting lying there all tangled up in cord and laundry. Sort of like a bound captive waiting for her new lord and master after a raid."

For an instant she just stared up at him in shock and then, to his astonishment, genuine fury erupted in her eyes. "Why you rotten, two-bit bastard. You lousy son of a—"

"Hey, I was just teasing," he interrupted quickly, reaching down to assist her. He'd been prepared for fireworks, but certainly not this degree of real anger. She looked as if she hated him in that moment.

"I should have expected that kind of humor from you," Rachel blazed as he helped her to her feet. She shook off his hand, endeavoring to free herself of the line and wet clothes without further assistance. "A man like you *would* think this was funny."

"A man like me?"

"I wouldn't expect you to have any human empathy or understanding or even a certain amount of good manners. You're nothing but a self-centered, ruthless—"

"Rachel!" He made his voice cold and abrupt in an attempt to cut through the tirade.

She blinked, as if she'd just realized what she was saying. Chance could almost see her reestablishing her self-control. Gradually her eyes cleared, the fire in her gaze diminishing rapidly as she got hold of herself. It was a fascinating process to watch. Chance got the impression Rachel didn't lose control very often.

"I think I can see why Mrs. Vinson felt this job was on a par with being shipped off to Siberia," Rachel muttered, bending down to pick up muddy clothing.

"Rachel, the bit about you looking like a bound captive was just a joke," Chance said, uncertain of her mood. "You're not hurt, are you?"

"No, I am not hurt." She continued picking up dirty laundry. "If you'll excuse me, I'll get back to work."

Chance stepped forward and put out a hand to touch her, unconsciously wanting to soothe her. "I'll help you with that laundry."

"Don't bother. This is my job, remember?" She twisted aside to avoid his hand and started to stalk past him with an armful of muddy clothes. Chance had the impression she wanted to escape.

Without pausing to think about what he was doing, Chance reached out and snagged her before she could dodge, pulling Rachel abruptly back toward him.

She found herself trapped against his chest and, when she lifted her face to tell him how little she liked the position, Chance lowered his head and kissed her.

3

RACHEL WAS SO STARTLED at the unexpected impact of Chance's kiss that for a breathless instant she stood perfectly still. Her blazing temper was suddenly chilled to ice. She had time to acknowledge the heat of his mouth and the slow, deliberate manner in which he was learning the feel and taste of her, and then a strange panic blossomed within her.

This was all wrong. *This was what he had done to Gail.* Rachel began to struggle fiercely, but Chance's hold on her was already far too secure. She could barely move inside the hard, unyielding circle of his arms. The strength in him overwhelmed her as he tightened his grasp and pinned her against his chest.

"Calm down, you little wildcat," Chance said into her mouth as she strained to get away from him. "I'm kissing you, not beating you. After the way you yelled at me a minute ago, you're lucky to get off this lightly."

There was an indulgent humor in his words that further infuriated her. "Let go of me, Chance, or so help me, I'll—"

"You'll what?" he asked tauntingly. "Pack your things and leave? Be my guest. I don't recall inviting you here in the first place. And I've already explained that the men in my family don't take well to ultimatums from their women. Don't make threats you aren't prepared to carry out."

"I'm not one of your women," she snarled, seizing on the one thing he had said that had rekindled her anger and panic. "Do you hear me, Abraham Chance? *I am not one of your women.*"

"I hear you." He lifted his head long enough to look down into the sea-green fire of her eyes. "But are you listening to yourself? Don't you think you're overreacting to what was only a minor bit of teasing? It's not as if I pushed you into that fish pond. And it's not as if you're hurt. What the hell's the matter with you?"

Rachel flinched as the reality of what he was saying hit home. He was right. In his view she probably had overreacted. If she wasn't very careful he was going to start wondering what the real problem was. She could hardly explain that when she had found herself bound hand and foot with clothesline, lying helplessly at his feet, the image of being his prisoner had been far too real. It had reminded her of why she was here in this isolated spot in the first place, hanging damp laundry. It had reminded her of the real danger in the situation. All her instincts of self-defense had leaped to life.

This was her enemy. She must never forget that. But part of her, she knew now, was in danger of forgetting or ignoring or overlooking that basic fact. That was what had really enraged her. As she had lain there in the mud looking up at him, watching him laugh, hearing his light taunts, she had known a rush of frustrated fury that had erupted before she could control herself.

If she had any hope of finding a way to avenge herself on this man, she had to get herself in hand first. A few more incidents like this one and Chance would become suspicious.

Rachel gave herself a tiny shake and drew a deep breath. She could still feel the steel in his arms, but she stopped struggling against it. Instantly his hold became warm and solid and reassuring. She was no longer trapped in a vise. She managed a tremulous smile.

"Sorry," she got out with gratifying smoothness and just the right touch of sophisticated chagrin. "I'm afraid I lost my temper because of my own carelessness. When you made a joke out of the whole thing I vented my anger on you. It was a dumb thing to do." She swallowed and then said politely, "I apologize for the nasty cracks about you and your sense of humor."

The hard line of his mouth eased into a faint smile, although his eyes remained dangerously watchful. "Apology accepted. You have my apology for the bound-slave comment."

"Professional housekeepers are very touchy about slave jokes," Rachel said. "They come a little too close to home."

"I hadn't thought of that. Do you think of your job as being the next step up from slavery?"

"Well, I suppose it's not as bad as being a wife. At least I get paid for my work. And I don't have to tolerate sexual advances from management."

His gaze darkened, and his fingers sank into the skin of her waist. "You are touchy, aren't you? I'd like to take this opportunity to point out that I don't usually go around kissing professional housekeepers."

"Why make an exception in my case?" she retorted.

"I don't know," he admitted grimly. "Something about you just interests me, I guess." His mouth came back down on hers.

This time Rachel was prepared. She stood stiffly in his grasp, but she didn't try to struggle. There was no point, and besides, she sensed he would release her soon enough when he found neither sensual response nor feminine challenge. As long as she didn't excite his predatory instincts, Rachel told herself, she would be safe.

His mouth moved on hers deliberately. There was a curious, seeking quality to his kiss this time, as though he were searching for answers. Rachel wondered what kind of questions he was asking. She could only hope he didn't yet suspect her real reason for playing this dangerous game. She was safe only as long as Chance didn't realize they were enemies.

"It's all right, Rachel," he muttered against her lips. His hands worked soothingly, sensually, on her spine. "It's okay. Just relax. Don't fight me. I won't hurt you. Trust me that much." The coaxing words were scattered like dark jewels against her skin as he tasted her with small, compelling kisses. "I just want to hold you for a few minutes. I've been wondering how you would feel in my arms."

She mustn't respond, Rachel warned herself. Yet it was dangerous to fight. She was left in an ambivalent state that didn't suit her temperament in the least. She was a woman of action. It was not her nature to endure without protest or to remain passive. She tried to ignore the inviting, intriguing quality of Chance's caresses, but something was flaring up inside her.

She hoped the aching emotion was restrained anger, but she was very much afraid it wasn't. Her body was beginning to burn, but it was not with fury. She could feel a vibrant awareness along her nerve endings, and she knew it was not the alertness of anger or even of fear. This was something else, something potentially devastating. Her hands came up instinctively to push against Chance's shoulders.

But when he felt her fingertips moving on him, Chance groaned and deepened the kiss. Suddenly he was inside her mouth, and Rachel knew it was because she had parted her lips for him. Instead of shoving at him, her hands tightened on the fabric of his shirt. Everything about him was impacting her senses now. She could smell the tang of honest sweat, feel the dynamic shift of muscle beneath her hands.

When Chance's hands moved downward to curve around her buttocks and pull her into the heat of his thighs, Rachel's mind began narrowing its focus. Thoughts of her stepsister and of her own plans faded temporarily beneath the growing need to learn more about this strange hunger. Rachel was feeling breathless and alive, longing for a fulfillment she refused to name, even to herself. Her head began to spin.

"Rachel?" Her name was both a hoarse question and a soft, urgent command. Chance reluctantly lifted his head to look down at her with smoky-gray eyes; the smoke was rapidly turning to flame. "I know this is happening a little too fast for you, but it's going to be okay, I promise. Believe me, I'm as surprised as you are. But some things in life just happen this way. Only a fool would walk away or ignore them."

His face was stark with a riveting sensual awareness. His whole body had grown hard with desire. Rachel caught her breath as she met his gaze. He wanted her. If she allowed it, he would take her here and now. The knowledge burned itself into her senses, and the soft, aching longing within her began to clamor for release.

A part of her screamed another warning. This was insane. She couldn't believe she had gotten herself into this situation. She must be out of her mind.

"Chance, please," she said, fumbling again for control and knowing she sounded desperate, "I didn't mean for this to happen. I don't want it to happen. It's all wrong. Please let me go."

"What are you afraid of, honey?" he asked gently. He drew one callused finger down the side of her throat. She shivered, but not with fear.

"You," she said baldly.

"There's no need to be afraid of me. Relax, and I'll show you." The blunt finger found the curve of her shoulder and then circled down to the delicate hollow of her throat. The touch was infinitely gentle and wholly male. Rachel shivered again and, when he felt the telltale reaction, Chance smiled.

It was the smile that gave Rachel the added impetus she needed to break the spell gathering around her. There was the knowledge of impending victory in that smile, she told herself. Chance was already anticipating his own satisfaction. She would not gratify his desire for conquest. She would not give him the kind of victory her stepsister had provided. Thoughts of Gail gave her courage.

"I asked you to let me go, Chance," she said with as much coolness as she could muster.

He hesitated for a long moment and then he released her. The expression in his eyes became unreadable once more. "I didn't mean to frighten you."

"I know."

"I'll fix the clothesline."

She drew a breath. "An excellent idea. You do that." Without another word she turned and walked toward the house. She didn't look back until she was safely indoors.

As she closed the back door behind her, Rachel realized she was shaking. She closed her eyes and summoned both her strength and her common sense.

She had come very close to disaster out there by the fish pond. If she stayed in this house much longer she would be increasing the risk. If she was smart she would leave right now. She had learned nothing useful during the past couple of days.

But she knew, even as she gave herself the lecture, that she was not going to walk away from Snowball's Chance. Not yet.

The ringing of the telephone jarred her out of her uneasy state. She opened her eyes and wondered which of Chance's many demanding associates she would have to get rid of this time. When the phone rang again she went into the hall and answered it.

"Snowball's Chance," she said politely.

There was a brief pause on the other end of the line, as if whoever had placed the call was having trouble adjusting to the fact that a woman had answered. "May I speak to Abraham Chance, please?" a male voice finally asked.

"I'm sorry, Mr. Chance is unable to come to the phone. I'm his housekeeper. Can I take a message?"

There was a sigh on the other end of the line. "So he's got someone else to answer his phone for him now, huh? Well, it's better than having the receiver slammed down in my ear. I'd better introduce myself, because we'll probably get to know each other fairly well. I intend to keep calling until I get an appointment with Chance, and you'll probably have to keep telling me he isn't available. I'm Keith Braxton."

Braxton. The name rang a bell. "You're the free-lance writer who's trying to do a story on Chance."

"I see he's already warned you about me. What's the man's problem, anyway?" An aggressive, almost hostile tone momentarily clouded the pleasant quality of

Keith Braxton's voice. Instantly it was smoothed away. "What's he got against a little free publicity?"

Rachel wondered about that herself. "Maybe he doesn't need any free publicity."

"That's not what I hear. I got the impression he was thinking of starting his own security firm. At least that's what one of the secretaries at Dixon Security let slip."

"I'm afraid I don't know anything about Chance's plans. I told you I'm just his housekeeper."

"You don't sound like a housekeeper."

"Is that right?" For some reason she was miffed. She'd done a heck of a lot of hard housekeeping during the past couple of days.

"Are you really the housekeeper?"

"I just finished doing a ton of laundry, and soon I'm going to have to wash about forty windows. Believe me, I feel exactly like a housekeeper."

Braxton chuckled. "Okay, okay, I believe you. Hey, any chance you might be willing to talk to me?"

Rachel held her breath as a whole new realm of possibilities opened up to her. "Talk to you? You want to pump me about my employer?"

"Don't worry," Braxton said hastily, "I'm not asking for any breach of professional housekeeping ethics." His voice became coaxing. "I'd just like to talk to you. I'd be willing to pay you for your time."

Rachel gripped the phone. "I don't know. I'm very busy, and I don't know if I can spare the time."

"I pay well. How does fifty bucks for an hour of your time sound? That's got to be a heck of a lot more than

housekeeping pays. I just want some background in
formation, not state secrets."

"That's good, because I don't know any state secrets." Rachel hesitated a moment longer. Visions of her
unexpected vulnerability out by the fish pond assailed
her. Along with the visions came a resurgence of her
anger. She took the plunge. "All right, Mr. Braxton. I'll
talk to you. Where shall we meet?"

He named a restaurant on the outskirts of the town
Rachel automatically reached for a pen and jotted the
name of the cafe on a pad of paper near the phone.

"I'll throw in a free lunch," Braxton concluded in-
gratiatingly. "See you around noon."

"I'll be there," Rachel promised rashly. But her anger was fading, and she was already beginning to have
second thoughts. This business of trying to take revenge was full of pitfalls and perilous decisions. She
had never attempted anything like this before in her life,
and every step forward was a step into the unknown.

She hung up the phone when Braxton bade her a
cheerful goodbye, and then she stood staring down at
the name of the restaurant she'd written on the pad of
paper.

If Keith Braxton wanted to do a story on Chance, he
might be just the tool she needed. She could give Braxton all sorts of information about how Chance operated. She could tell him how he'd devastated her
stepsister's life, how he'd then framed Gail for theft,
handed her over to the wolves and walked away. He
hadn't even bothered to find the solution to the crime

he'd been hired to solve in the first place. Chance had simply found a sacrificial victim and used her to make himself and Dixon Security look good.

The real story of how Abraham Chance operated might capture Keith Braxton's interest, and if it did, he might write an article tearing Chance to shreds. It would be a fitting vengeance.

Yes, she would meet Braxton tomorrow at the restaurant on the outskirts of town. Rachel reached out and tore the piece of paper off the pad. She crumpled it in her hand and started to throw it into the trash. Then she had second thoughts. No sense leaving evidence lying around. If Chance happened to see a crumpled note in the trash he might just be curious enough to glance at it.

Rachel shoved the wad of paper into the pocket of her jeans and went upstairs to take a shower. At least Chance had some redeeming virtues. He had gotten the hot water tank working again.

She knew she wanted to do more than wash off the mud from the fish pond. She wanted to try to wash away the feel of Chance's hands and the touch of his mouth.

CHANCE WAS GETTING RESTLESS. His patience was wearing thin. He didn't like secrets, and Rachel was definitely hiding a few. He was certainly not making much progress in getting her to confide in him. So much for the virtues of subtle persuasion. He'd known from the start it wasn't his forte.

All through dinner he'd been aware of Rachel's maintaining a cool distance. She was more wary than ever of him, it seemed. When he spoke to her she answered in short, clipped sentences, saying no more than was necessary. She made no effort to keep the conversation going. Usually during the dinner hour they talked about his plans for Snowball's Chance. Tonight she didn't have a single question for him.

Chance was not only feeling restless, he was beginning to feel annoyed. When Rachel got to her feet and began clearing the table, he finally decided to take stronger action.

He leaned back in his chair, stretching his legs out in front of him, and watched her move about the kitchen. "Are you going to sulk all evening because of that little scene at the fish pond?" he demanded.

Her head came around quickly, irritation and something that might have been alarm flaring in her gaze. "I'm not sulking. I'm working. It's what you're paying me for, isn't it? To work? I didn't know I was required to provide after-dinner entertainment."

Chance swore under his breath and drummed his fingers once on the tabletop in a trademark gesture of irritation. "Calm down. I just asked a simple question. It gets lonely up here at night. Somehow it seems lonelier sharing the house with someone who won't even speak to me."

"What do you want to talk about?" she asked reluctantly.

He smiled faintly. "Let's talk about you."

"Let's not."

"Why not?" Chance persisted smoothly. "Why are you so reluctant to tell me anything about yourself, Rachel?"

She busied herself with the sinkful of dishes. "What do you want to know?"

He must not rush this interrogation, Chance told himself firmly. He must go slowly and cautiously. He did not want her to know she was being grilled. "How long have you worked as a housekeeper?" he asked blandly.

"Not long."

He kept silent for a moment, hoping she would volunteer more information. When she didn't, he tried again. "Do you like the work?"

"Not particularly. But it's a job."

"And you need one?"

"Don't we all?"

This was getting him nowhere fast. "You said you had a sister."

"Yes." She gripped a slippery plate very tightly.

"What's her name?"

He could have sworn she was momentarily disconcerted by the simple question. "Anna," she finally mumbled.

She was lying, Chance thought in surprise. He wondered why. "Is Anna a lot younger than you?"

"Anna is only twenty. She's very young, very naive. Far too trusting."

"More trusting than you are?" Chance got to his feet and ambled over to the counter to pick up a towel. He began drying the dishes she was stacking.

"Unfortunately, yes, she is."

"Does it occur to you, Rachel, that you might be a little too untrusting?"

She slanted him a cool, derisive smile. "Are you implying I should trust you a little more than I do, Chance?"

Holding a dish in one hand and the towel in the other, he looked down at her. "I'd like that, Rachel."

"Yes," she said, "I'll just bet you would. Why don't you answer a few of my questions now?"

He stifled a sigh. "All right. What do you want to know?"

She blinked owlishly as if she hadn't expected him to be so agreeable. "Well, what are you going to do with Snowball's Chance when you get it fixed up?"

"Use it for weekends and vacations, probably. I won't be able to run my business from here, but it will make a great escape spot. I like coming up here into the mountains. Makes a nice break from the city and the kind of work I do."

"Do you like your work?"

"It has its satisfactions," he said with a shrug. "And a few frustrations."

"What kind of frustrations?"

He wondered at her sudden interest. "Sometimes things can't be settled to my satisfaction. Sometimes corporate politics get in the way of a good security investigation." He heard the bitterness in his own words and was annoyed. "I'm hoping that things will be a little different when I'm working for myself."

She gave him an odd look and seemed to run out of questions. Chance sought some way to keep her talking. "I unearthed an old box of checkers in a trunk out in the coach house today. Want to try a couple of games?"

"All right. There's not much else to do up here at night, is there?"

"Not unless we go back to doing what we were doing at the fish pond this afternoon," he agreed.

"Don't hold your breath," she shot back, but there was no real venom in her words.

"I won't."

A long time later Chance lay in bed and went over every nuance of his gentle attempt at interrogation. He hadn't learned much about Miss Rachel Wilder, just enough to tantalize himself and make him more curious than ever.

He had also learned it was tough to keep his mind on a verbal investigation when his body was demanding a much more intimate exploration. Chance stared into the darkness and admitted to himself just how much he wanted all of Rachel, now that he'd teased himself with a taste.

She had felt very good in his arms that afternoon. Soft and sensual and alive. And she had responded. She would probably never admit it, at least not now, but he had felt the shiver of awareness course through her.

Her mouth had opened beneath his, and part of her had definitely welcomed the deep intimacy of his kiss.

It was incredibly frustrating having to wonder why she was so determined to fight him. Chance decided he would like very much to get his hands on the man who had made Rachel Wilder so wary. Whoever he was, he was probably the reason she was hiding out here at Snowball's Chance.

The first thing he had to do, Chance knew, was to convince Rachel she was safe here. When he'd accomplished that much, he could proceed to step two.

Step two was to get her into his bed. He couldn't remember the last time he'd wanted a woman as badly as he was beginning to want Rachel Wilder.

Patience, he told himself grimly. He had to have patience.

CHANCE'S BID FOR PATIENCE was severely strained the next day, however, when he found the impressions on the notepad beside the telephone. The original note had been ripped off, but it wasn't difficult to read the indentations left by the pen.

Chance deciphered the familiar name of the restaurant and felt a slow burn begin somewhere deep inside. Rachel had left for town sometime earlier, telling him there was a sandwich waiting in the kitchen. She had said she had some shopping to do.

It was the first time she'd ever gone shopping during the noon hour. He had already been feeling abandoned, not looking forward to a lonely lunch. Strange how quickly he'd grown accustomed to her company. For a man who was used to being on his own, it was a weird feeling.

But the name of the restaurant on the notepad implied that Rachel was not dieting today.

It didn't take a great deal of investigative talent to figure out that his mysterious housekeeper was on her way to meet someone for lunch. Given the fact that she was a stranger in the vicinity, that raised some interesting questions.

Chance picked up the keys to the Chevy and stalked out the door. He was getting tired of asking questions about Rachel Wilder and not getting any answers. Maybe it was time to start conducting a more active investigation.

But as long as he was going to follow the lady to her rendezvous, he might as well take a load of junk to the local dump site. True, it wasn't a very large load, because most of the items he'd inventoried had appeared potentially useful. But there was a stack of empty cardboard boxes he could get rid of. He wanted to clear some space in the overcrowded coach house.

There was plenty of time for a short detour. After all, he knew exactly where Rachel was headed.

RACHEL WAS ALARMED by the terrible sense of guilt she was feeling as she parked her car in the restaurant lot. The guilt had set in shortly after the phone call from Keith Braxton and her rash promise to meet him for lunch. It hadn't taken her long to regret her decision, but when she'd thought about canceling the lunch she had realized she had no phone number for Braxton. She didn't even know where he was staying. She had spent a restless night trying to think of a way to explain her change of heart to the journalist.

She couldn't even explain it to herself. She just knew that this wasn't the kind of revenge she wanted.

She dropped her keys into her purse and headed toward the door of the restaurant, rehearsing her apologies.

Keith Braxton was waiting for her in the restaurant lobby. He had an open, pleasant face with handsome features and warm brown eyes. He was about her age with hair a few shades lighter than her own, and he was dressed casually in jeans and pullover. He came forward with an extended hand and a cheerful, engaging smile.

"You must be Rachel. I'm Keith Braxton, and I can't tell you how glad I am you agreed to meet me today. Doing research on Abraham Chance is like pulling teeth on a chicken."

"I can imagine it would be twice as difficult without the cooperation of the chicken," Rachel said politely as the hostess showed them to a table near the window.

"You can say that again," Braxton muttered with great depth of feeling. "The man's about as cooperative as a stone. You'd think I was trying to do a big exposé or something."

Rachel looked at him. "Exactly what are you trying to do?"

"Just a profile of one of today's top-notch business security investigators." Braxton leaned forward, his eyes alight with enthusiasm. "They're a whole new breed, Rachel. They combine the gut instincts of the old-fashioned private eye with all the new techniques needed to track down today's white collar criminal. They don't mess around with divorce and custody cases. They go after embezzlers and computer thieves. Vast sums of money are often involved. Sometimes the agencies provide bodyguard services for high-powered executives who are worth their weight in ransom. They handle tricky courier transfers and provide expertise and advice to companies trying to tighten up internal security. Corporations are willing to pay well for the services, and the really good operatives, like Chance, can name their price." Braxton sat back as the menus were delivered.

"And you want to do an article on Chance because he's one of the best in the field, is that it?"

"Right. I'm not surprised to hear Chance is leaving Dixon Security to go out on his own. My research tells me he's got the business sense as well as the investigative ability to start his own agency. He's the perfect subject for an article on the profession. I really want to do this story. I'm sure I can sell it. The personal touch is going to be dynamite."

"I see." Rachel opened her menu, staring blindly at the list of items in front of her. This, she decided, had been a really stupid idea.

Maybe, with a certain degree of effort, she could sway Braxton's opinion of Chance and get him portrayed as a cunning, malicious man. But that wasn't the way she wanted to go. She remembered the burning intimacy of Chance's kiss the previous afternoon and knew that any vengeance she took had to be as intimate and devastating as that kiss. She didn't want to even the score by the conniving, manipulative use of a third party.

Vengeance was a very personal thing, she was learning. As personal as passion.

"Well, Rachel? What do you say? Will you give me a hand?"

She decided to tell him the truth immediately. "I'm afraid I'm not going to be of much help to you, Keith. I just work for the man, and I've only been at Snowball's Chance for a few days. Not long enough to learn any of his secrets. I wanted to call you back yesterday and cancel this appointment, but I didn't have your number."

For an instant his pleasant expression turned into a look of cold fury. The anger came and went so quickly in his eyes that Rachel wasn't even positive she'd seen it. But she was left with an unnerving impression of having come very close to seeing another side of the pleasant-faced, easygoing journalist.

"I've been tracking Chance for weeks," Braxton muttered tightly.

Rachel nodded uneasily. "I understand. It's just that I can't talk about him. It wouldn't be right."

"I had a feeling you were going to say that," Keith said with a sigh. "The minute I saw you I knew you weren't going to sell any of Chance's secrets for a lousy fifty bucks."

"It's not his secrets you want. You said you wanted to do a profile, an interview," she protested.

"True, but the odds of getting one are getting slimmer by the day." Braxton gave her an assessing glance. "I don't suppose you could put in a good word for me?"

Rachel was startled. "I don't know. I hadn't thought about it. Frankly, if he found out I had lunch with you, he'd probably snap my head off. I'm not sure I'd last long enough to put in any kind of word for you."

"Got a temper, huh?"

Rachel smiled. "I haven't witnessed it, but I have a hunch he does. Look, Keith, I'm sorry to have wasted your time today."

"Forget it. It's nice to have a companion for lunch."

"You still want to buy me lunch?"

He grinned. "There's not a whole heck of a lot to do in this town. I was about to give up and go home tomorrow, anyway. When I got you on the phone yesterday, I thought I'd make one last try for some kind of story. But you're right. Nothing short of an interview with Chance himself would really do the trick. Guess I'll just have to find someone else in the business to profile."

"I appreciate the lunch," Rachel said with a relieved smile. Braxton was going to be nice about this, after all.

"It makes a nice break from washing walls and scrubbing floors."

Braxton laughed. "I can't say I blame you. But I've got to tell you that you sure don't look like any housekeeper I ever met."

"I'm discovering a lot of people seem to have a very old-fashioned image of the profession."

"Well, if we're not going to talk about Abraham Chance," Keith Braxton said cheerfully, "what shall we discuss?"

"You don't happen to know the name of a good window-washing firm here in town, do you? I'm thinking of subcontracting out some of my job responsibilities."

Keith chuckled good-naturedly. "This must be your lucky day. You won't believe the sign I saw in a window down the street. Something along the lines of We Do Windows."

"You're right. This must be my lucky day."

"What do you say we have lunch and then I'll show you the place." Keith raised his hand to signal the waitress, but in the process he accidentally knocked over his glass of water. The liquid spilled over the tabletop and ran off into Rachel's lap.

"Oh, dear." Rachel jumped to her feet, dabbing at the water.

"Sorry about that," Keith said apologetically. He handed her a napkin. "I think you're going to need more than this. Why don't you use the towels in the rest room?"

He was right. She was going to need more than a paper napkin. Rachel regarded her soaked pants with resignation. "I'll be right back." Maybe this wasn't going to be her lucky day, after all, she thought morosely as she headed for the ladies' room.

It was definitely not Abraham Chance's lucky day. Rachel found him on the floor of the old coach house an hour later when she returned to Snowball's Chance.

At first glance she thought he was dead.

4

CHANCE WAS NOT DEAD, but one look at the rusted hulk of an ancient automobile radiator that lay beside him told Rachel he easily could have been killed. The heavy chunk of metal had apparently fallen from the loft above, dealing Chance a glancing blow. A scant inch closer, and the falling metal wouldn't have grazed his head and shoulder. It would have crushed his skull.

"Chance! Oh, my God, are you all right?" Rachel raced toward his prone body. Chance was sprawled on the dusty floor of the coach house amid a bunch of old cardboard boxes. Blood streaked his face and arm. He stirred groggily when he heard her voice, and he opened his eyes.

"No," he said in a slightly blurred, wholly annoyed voice, "I am not all right. My head is spinning, and my arm hurts. I may be sick to my stomach."

"Don't move." She crouched down beside him, shaken by the dazed expression in his normally alert eyes. She touched the wound on his head with careful fingers. There was plenty of blood, but the gash didn't look deep.

"I wasn't planning on running any marathons. Ouch!"

"I'm sorry. I just wanted to see how bad the cut is. There's enough blood to terrorize the average innocent bystander such as me, but the wound itself doesn't look all that bad." She tried to keep her voice light and soothing.

"Head wounds always bleed a lot," he muttered, blinking groggily as he tried to sit up. "I read that somewhere."

Rachel put out a restraining hand. "Wait, I'll call an ambulance."

"Forget the ambulance. I'm not that bad. I just need to get cleaned up and rest for a while. Something tells me I'm going to have a splitting headache."

Rachel hesitated. "I think we should get a doctor's verdict."

"Not necessary."

It was time to take a firm hand. Chance was obviously going to be a difficult patient. Rachel slipped into her most polished, assertive managerial voice. "I say it is necessary." She steadied him as he struggled to his feet. "You can play macho man some other time. I'm the housekeeper around here, and that puts me in charge of situations like this."

"Is that right?" He gazed down at her with an expression that should have been twice as forbidding as usual because of all the gore on his face. But somehow he just managed to look only mildly ferocious. Chance was definitely not in top form.

"Yes, that's right. You're in no condition to make major decisions. Come on. If you don't want an ambulance I'll compromise. I'll take you into town to see a doctor."

"Geez. Just what I needed. A bossy, assertive female."

"Don't tell me. The men of the Chance family don't like assertive women any better than they like women who give ultimatums, right?" She staggered beneath his weight as he braced himself against her shoulder.

"Not true. Assertive women," Chance declared consideringly, "can be interesting. Have I ever told you I like the feisty type?"

"That's a very open-minded attitude." It was taking all her strength to get him to the passenger side of the Toyota. The man seemed to weigh a ton.

"I am a very open-minded man."

"That's very reassuring." She groaned as she finally let his weight slide from her shoulders down onto the passenger seat. She frowned worriedly as she started to close the car door. "Chance, maybe I should call that ambulance instead."

"No." His voice was stronger. "I promise you it looks worse than it is."

Rachel shook her head and got behind the wheel. "What happened in the coach house?" she asked as she swung the car back out of the drive. "How long have you been lying in there?"

"Beats me." Chance slouched in his corner, watching her through narrowed, bleary eyes as she drove. Then he remembered to glance at his watch. "I was headed for the car about—" he frowned, trying to read the dial "—about twenty minutes ago. So I couldn't have been in there very long. I don't think I was unconscious, just badly dazed for a few minutes. It was a while before I felt like moving, and then I heard your car in the drive."

"But what happened?"

"For the past few days I've been sorting through the stuff in the coach house. You know that. Today I'd planned to take a load of junk to the dump."

"What load of junk? Yesterday when I took a look in the coach house, I saw absolutely nothing but a few cardboard boxes in the discard pile. As far as I could tell you're keeping everything you come across in there. You're a regular pack rat. You probably missed your calling, Chance. You should have opened up a junkyard."

"The stuff I'm keeping is not junk. It's valuable, useful equipment," he retorted forcefully. The effort of defending his coach-house collection made him wince. His hand went to his head, and he gritted his teeth.

"Most of it looks like junk to me, but never mind." She slanted him a worried glance. "Are you sure you're okay?"

"I'm okay." He lowered his hand and absently wiped the blood off on his jeans. "I guess I must have moved some stuff in the loft earlier that was supporting something heavy. It must have been poised to fall, and I was just unlucky enough to be under it when it did."

"It looked like a car radiator."

"Hmm. Yeah. Could be." He brightened noticeably. "There was an old one stored up there. A real nice one that probably belonged to a '57 Chevy. Looked like all it needed was flushing out and maybe a little patching. I was going to store it downstairs, but I hadn't gotten around to moving it from the loft yet."

"Store it! Chance, what would you want with an old radiator for a '57 Chevy?"

"Are you kidding? Original equipment for that kind of car is worth a lot of cash."

"I give up. All right, so you think it just toppled over on you?"

"It must have been sitting precariously up there waiting for the slightest movement to knock it down. When I went in there today I probably jarred one of the posts that holds up the loft, with just enough force to make the radiator fall over the edge." He paused for a moment and then added quietly, "Although I don't remember hitting any of the posts. I was just going to collect some cardboard boxes." He shrugged and winced again.

Rachel's hands clenched and unclenched around the wheel. She stared straight ahead. "You were very lucky," was all she said. She wondered why she was so concerned. Theoretically she was supposed to be nursing a fierce anger toward this man. Yet all she could think about was that he was hurt and had very nearly been killed. Her stomach was in a knot.

"I know." He frowned intently as if trying to recall something. "It must have made some noise when it started to fall. Probably scraped the edge of the loft floor or something."

"Why do you say that?"

"Because I heard a sound just before the lights went out. I remember thinking something was wrong and that I had to move. Instinct, I guess."

"You probably moved just enough to save your life."

"A miss is as good as a mile," he said a little too blithely. He closed his eyes and leaned his head back against the headrest.

Rachel shuddered. "Barely."

"Did you get what you needed in town?" The question came quietly.

"Yes." She concentrated on her driving.

He opened one eye. "Where are your packages? I don't see any."

Rachel began to grow uneasy. She shot him a quick, assessing glance. There was considerably more alertness in that smoky gaze now than there had been a few minutes ago. Chance was recovering rapidly. "I didn't buy anything. I just made some arrangements."

"Arrangements?"

"For some work I want done at Snowball's Chance."

"What kind of arrangements were you making?" He sounded vaguely alarmed. "I'm the one who hires people to work at Snowball's Chance."

Her uneasiness grew. "I'll explain it all later."

"Good," Chance said with soft emphasis. "I'd like to hear a few explanations from you."

He closed his eyes and didn't say another word until they reached the small clinic in town. Rachel had the unsettling feeling she had just had some sort of reprieve.

The doctor's verdict was reassuring. No, he didn't think Chance was seriously injured. A possible mild concussion, and the scrape on his shoulder required a stitch or two, but that was it. Because Chance had suffered a head injury, he was instructed to spend the next day or so in bed. He didn't take well to the instructions.

He started protesting the moment they left the doctor's office, continued the protests while Rachel filled a pain prescription at the local pharmacy and kept up his arguments all the way back to Snowball's Chance.

"I just need a couple of hours of rest," he informed her as she helped him upstairs to his room an hour later.

"The doctor said two days in bed, and that's what you're going to get."

"He just meant I should take things easy."

"The easiest way to take things easy is in bed."

"Depends what a man wants to take." His eyes were growing clearer and more alert by the minute.

Rachel shifted uncomfortably under that gleaming gaze. "Save the wisecracks for later. Right now you're going to get some rest."

"Are all housekeepers this bossy?"

"Goes with the territory," she assured him.

Once she had him in his bedroom she halted, not sure what to do next. She glanced toward the old double bed, which was covered with an aging quilt.

Chance leered at her pleasantly. "Going to stick around and help me undress?"

"I get the feeling you can handle that much yourself."

"Coward." His hands went to the first button of his jeans.

"I'll go downstairs and fix you some soup," Rachel said quickly, and made a fast exit.

Chance watched her leave while he automatically unfastened his jeans. She was definitely aware of him now in the way that a woman is aware of a man. He was making progress. She was not stupid, he decided as he stepped out of his dusty jeans. She might try to ignore the physical attraction that was sizzling between them, but she knew perfectly well it existed.

Something crinkled in the pocket of his jeans. Chance remembered the slip of notepaper and reached inside to pull it out. Thoughtfully he smoothed the piece of paper and studied the indentations that spelled out the name of the restaurant. Rachel hadn't mentioned having lunch while she was in town making her "arrangements." He wondered what sort of story he would hear if he confronted her with the evidence.

He would think about that later, Chance decided. Right now he was tired. Far more tired than he wanted to acknowledge. His arm ached, and his head hurt. He headed for the bed.

He awoke twice during the night, each time to the unfamiliar sensation of a woman's hand on his brow. He didn't have to open his eyes to know who stood beside his bed, checking him for signs of fever.

The first time he pretended not to awaken, preferring to luxuriate in the sensation of being coddled by Rachel Wilder. She hovered over him for several minutes, her light robe making whispery sounds in the darkness. The warm, feminine scent of her filled his nostrils when she leaned across him to adjust his blanket. His whole body went taut in reaction. When he felt the brush of her arm, he was sorely tempted to reach up and pull her down into bed. It took all his willpower to resist.

The sound of the door being cautiously opened alerted him the second time she came into the room. This time he took the risk of watching her through half-closed eyes. She had tied the sash of her robe with a casual knot that loosened suddenly when she leaned over him to straighten the quilt. For a tantalizing moment the pale moonlight gave Chance a brief glimpse of her nipples pushing against the fabric of her nightgown. The curve of her upper thigh was very close to his hand. That time he very nearly did reach out to drag her down beside him.

Rachel, he thought as she left the room, the hem of her robe floating out behind her, *what secrets are you hiding? Come here and tell me, honey. Your secrets, whatever they are, are safe with me.* Discovering the truth about Rachel Wilder was rapidly becoming the most important thing in his life. He had told himself again and again to be patient, but he wasn't sure how much longer he could exercise restraint.

Maybe it was time to try a bit more forcefulness.

The third time Chance awoke, sunlight was streaming in through the window, and the sound of voices drifted up the stairs. He lay still for a moment trying to figure out who would be visiting. The thought that whoever was downstairs might be a friend of Rachel's made him uneasy. Chance realized he didn't want anyone getting in the way of his investigation of Rachel.

"Rachel!" He shoved aside the covers and got to his feet, vastly relieved to discover he didn't have a headache.

The voices downstairs halted abruptly. Then Rachel spoke from the bottom of the stairs. "I'll be right up with your breakfast, Chance."

He stalked over to the window in time to see a young man with a long-handled brush and a pail of suds come around the side of the house and begin to clean a window. Chance had never seen the man before in his life.

When Rachel appeared a few minutes later holding a trayful of eggs and toast, Chance glared at her from the window. "Who the hell is that?"

Her eyes went wide and became glued to his nude figure. Hastily she started to back out of the room. "The window washers," she explained in an unnaturally high voice. "Yesterday when I was in town I arranged for them to come today."

"Damn it, Rachel, I hired you to do things like clean windows. I didn't give you a blank check to hire anyone else to help you. Why didn't you consult me about this? If you can't handle the job, you should have told me so. You've got no business going behind my back and arranging for assistance."

She disappeared out into the hall. "Put some clothes on, Chance."

"Get in here, Rachel, I'm trying to talk to you."

"I'm not coming back into that room until you're decent."

Thoroughly irritated, he started for the door. "Get in here and explain yourself, woman. I don't have an unlimited amount of cash to pour into this place, you know. My mother and sister inherited Dad's money. All I got was this house, remember? I've got to watch every penny that goes into this place. There isn't room in the budget for a lot of extras." He flung open the door and stood in the doorway, glaring at her.

"For heaven's sake, Chance! There are strangers here in the house!" She kept her eyes firmly fixed on his face.

"There wouldn't be any strangers here if you hadn't invited them. I hope you're prepared to pay the bill for those window washers."

"I refuse to discuss the matter further until you've had the good manners to put on some clothes." She tilted her chin and whirled around to start for the stairs.

"Come back here!"

"Not until you're dressed."

"All right, all right," he exploded, striding back into his bedroom and snatching a pair of clean jeans out of the closet. "I'm dressed," he snapped as he fastened the denims. "Now get in here and tell me what the hell you think you're doing running through my money as if it were water."

She came through the doorway, watching him warily. "It's a question of cost effectiveness," she declared briskly as she put the tray down on a nearby table. "I decided that in the long run it would be cheaper and more efficient to pay professionals to clean all these windows. This isn't a normal job, Chance. The grime on that glass has been accumulating for years. It would take me days to clean them properly, and I would have to spend money on the right equipment. The men who arrived this morning are experts. They'll have the whole house done in a couple of hours."

"While you do what?" he asked sullenly, his eyes on the eggs and toast. There was a steaming pot of coffee on the tray, and the lure of it was irresistible.

"Any one of a hundred other things that need doing around here. Now are you going to stand there complaining, or are you going to eat your breakfast?"

"It's a tough choice."

"Well, allow me to make it for you, then," she retorted far too sweetly. She scooped up the tray and started for the door again.

"Wait!" He reached out to stop her. "I'll eat, I'll eat."

"Good." With a smile of satisfaction, she set the tray down once more. "A wise decision."

He picked up a slice of toast while she poured his coffee. "Why not? I can always go back to complaining later."

She ignored that and sat down in a chair to watch him eat. "I'll be glad to give you a complete cost breakdown justifying my decision to hire the window washers."

"You sound like somebody's accountant or administrative assistant," he muttered. He didn't miss her small start of alarm when he said that, but he pretended not to notice. One more piece of the puzzle that was Rachel. He mentally stored it away. "Forget the cost breakdown. The window washers are here now, so they might as well finish the job."

"I like a man who knows when he's beaten."

He glanced up at that and was half amused by the unmistakable air of feminine superiority he saw in her eyes. Rachel certainly did have great eyes. His mouth twitched as he struggled to hide a smile. "It looks like you're also good at kicking a man while he's down. You know I'm not up to doing battle with you today."

"Does that mean you're going to spend the day in bed as the doctor ordered?"

"Not exactly."

She sighed. "I was afraid of that. You really should, you know. You took a nasty blow from that radiator yesterday."

"I'll survive. If it makes you feel any better, I promise to stick to light work today."

"Just so long as you don't bother the window washers."

He swore softly under his breath as he picked up his fork. "I thought I'd spend my time supervising you instead. Be interesting to see exactly how a professional housekeeper spends her time. Who knows? Maybe I'll pick up some lessons in the efficient use of time and motion."

"Who knows?" she agreed dryly. "Maybe you will. When you're through with breakfast bring the tray downstairs, and I'll put you to work polishing some old silver I found in a cupboard."

"Polishing silver! I've got better things to do with my time."

"Not today you don't. You're going to take it easy. You promised." She got to her feet and walked toward the door. "Besides, I think you'll look cute in an apron."

"You've got nerve, lady, I'll grant you that."

"You ain't seen nothin' yet," she vowed as she exited the room.

"No," Chance murmured to himself. He remembered the glimpse of her breasts that he'd had in the middle of the night and the warm, womanly scent of her body as she'd leaned over him. "I haven't seen it all yet, but I will. I promise you that, Rachel Wilder, I definitely will see everything. And I'm going to make it all mine. I'm going to unlock every secret you have. It's time you and I got much more closely acquainted."

Having made that decision, Chance went back to his breakfast.

The day passed with surprising swiftness. Rachel knew Chance was occasionally irritated and made restless by his enforced confinement, but he found plenty of quiet, indoor projects that needed doing. For the most part he stayed occupied and uncomplaining. After due consideration she decided to refrain from trying to put him into an apron. One could only push this man so far.

The window washers left shortly before lunch, and Rachel surveyed the results with a certain amount of satisfaction. The windows of the old house gleamed in the clear mountain sunlight. Even Chance seemed reasonably content with the success of the job. He also seemed to find her satisfaction amusing.

"Makes a big difference, doesn't it?" Rachel enthused as she stood on the front porch examining the clean windows. "There must have been ten years of grime on that glass. Just wait until you get those upper balconies fixed and put a coat of paint on this place."

"I told you the house was basically solid. Just needs a little love and attention, that's all. Not unlike some people I know."

She caught his coolly perusing glance and turned away from it. She didn't care for that particular expression in his eyes, and she thought she was seeing it more and more frequently lately. For an instant she wondered if he knew who she was but then she dismissed the concern. There was no way he could know she was related to Gail Vaughan.

"Some people," she said quietly, "can be kinder to a house than they are to other human beings."

"Are you trying to tell me something, Rachel?" he asked with lazy interest.

She flushed. "No, of course not. I was just making an observation. Well," she went on brightly, brushing her hands against her thighs, "are you ready for lunch?"

"I'm ready." He followed her into the house.

"Are you sure you feel all right?"

"I feel fine, Rachel."

"I'll believe that after you've had another night's sleep. You still look a little peaked."

"No, I don't."

"Yes, you do. You'd better check that loft carefully before you start working in the coach house again. There might be some other heavy objects up there that aren't properly secured."

"Yes, Rachel."

She heard the dry amusement in his voice and turned to glare at him. "Are you laughing at me?"

"Never." His virtuous expression was too good to be true.

Rachel's eyes narrowed slightly. "You find me amusing, don't you?"

"Sometimes," he admitted. "Mostly I just find you very interesting."

The comment was hardly reassuring.

She busied herself cleaning out some old closets for the rest of the day. Chance tried to give her a hand, but she quickly dismissed him.

"Go back to work on the silver," she ordered when he contradicted her decision to throw away an old wool coat that probably dated from the forties. "You're no help at all with this sort of thing. If you had your way you'd keep everything we find."

"That's not true, I just don't want to toss out anything useful."

"Hah. You don't know the meaning of the word 'useful.' Everything looks potentially 'useful' to you. Remember that huge pile of newspapers you wanted to save earlier? No one but a pack rat would save ten years' worth of twenty-year-old newspapers."

"Old newspapers are interesting," he protested. "They've got historical value."

"They were falling apart! They crumbled in your hand when you tried to open them, remember? Here. Put this coat in the sack with the papers and then go polish silver. That silver is definitely worth saving. Tomorrow you can return to the coach house. I'll never get through this place with you dogging my heels, fussing over everything I'm trying to throw away."

"So it might take a little longer with me helping you. What's the big deal? Are you in a hurry to finish here at Snowball's Chance, Rachel?"

"I don't want you to waste your money and my time," she mumbled, quickly folding the old coat. "You told me yourself you only wanted a housekeeper for a month. I can't stay here forever, you know."

"Got another housekeeping assignment lined up after this one?" Chance asked calmly as he took the coat from her.

She caught her breath. She wasn't all that good at thinking up lies on the spur of the moment, she realized. "I have other assignments waiting for me, yes."

"Going to spend the rest of your life taking care of other people's houses?"

Her hand stilled on an old package wrapped in brown paper and string that had been stored years ago and long since forgotten. She kept her gaze fixed on it as she answered Chance's question. "Who knows? People make career changes all the time."

"Somehow you seem like the kind of woman who always knows where she wants to be and what she'll be doing five or ten or twenty years from now."

"I don't have a crystal ball."

"Who does? Might be useful on occasion."

Something in his voice made her glance back over her shoulder. "What would you do with a crystal ball?"

His eyes locked with hers. "Ask some questions."

"About the past or the future?"

"Both." He broke the eye contact first, turning to stride down the hall with the old wool coat in his hands.

Rachel watched him go, her own mind filled with far too many questions. Through the sparkling-clean windows she could see the sky darkening with clouds as another rainstorm moved in.

THE HOUSE HAD BEEN DARK and quiet for several hours before Rachel finally acknowledged that she wasn't going to get to sleep very easily that night. The rain was now a steady drone outside. At least this storm was a relatively quiet one. Rachel didn't miss the thunder and lightning of that other storm, the one that had arrived the same night she had.

But the quiet beat of the rain wasn't having a soporific effect. She had worked hard that day, just as she had every day since she'd come to Snowball's Chance. She ought to be exhausted. Yet she was lying there with a head full of questions and a restless, uneasy feeling that was rapidly becoming far too familiar.

She had to face the fact that she wasn't making much headway in her search for revenge. Instead the man on whom she wanted to unleash vengeance was getting a lot of hard work out of her. Rachel's mouth twisted wryly. There was something wrong with this equation. She wondered what was the matter with her.

It was almost as if she were losing her desire to punish Chance.

But, then, it was hard to think of punishing a man who was nursing a bruised and battered body and a possible concussion. It was difficult to think about wreaking vengeance on a man who got excited over stacks of old newspapers and who lovingly saved every item of junk he came across in this house. It was almost impossible to scheme to crush a man who spent his evenings with her talking about his plans for the future. It was hard to plot revenge against a man who made it obvious just how much he wanted a home of his own.

She should have suspected something was going wrong when she couldn't bring herself to use Keith Braxton to get at Chance.

Or perhaps when she had found herself responding to Chance's kiss.

Chance's kiss.

That thought made her wonder how he was faring tonight. He had gone to bed earlier than usual, which had caused her to worry about him. She had seen him massaging his neck as he'd walked heavily up the stairs.

Rachel hoped he wasn't going to have some sort of relapse. She'd heard somewhere that head wounds could be deceptive. Maybe she ought to check him for signs of fever, as she had last night.

Tossing aside the covers, Rachel stood up on the cold floor. One of these days, she thought as she shivered, Chance was going to have to consider putting in new central heating. The old furnace was obviously on its last legs.

Even as she hurried barefoot down the hall to Chance's room, Rachel acknowledged that her concern about future plans for Snowball's Chance made no sense. By rights she should be concentrating on destroying the one thing Chance seemed to care about most at the moment.

The thought appalled her. She could no more do something terrible to Snowball's Chance than she could turn over its owner's secrets to a writer such as Keith Braxton.

That realization nearly stunned her as she reached the doorway of Chance's bedroom. The door stood open. Across the room she could see his shadowed form on the bed.

Perhaps she would never find the courage to take her revenge.

Slowly, as if drawn by an invisible string, Rachel walked toward the bed. She felt trapped in a dangerous web of emotions that she didn't fully understand. This was the man she thought she hated, the man she'd come to punish.

But the only clear impressions she had tonight were of the memory of his burning kiss and the shock of finding him hurt and bloodied yesterday. One memory still had the power to arouse an almost painful longing within her. The other made her want to offer comfort and care.

She must be out of her mind. She couldn't be falling in love with Chance. It was utterly impossible. *Impossible.*

She took another few steps toward the bed, unaware of the chilled floor now. She was disoriented, caught between two parallel realities. This was insane. This was crazy. She had to get a grip on herself and her wild, jumbled emotions. She was only here tonight to check him for fever.

"It's about time you got here," Chance murmured with sleepy satisfaction as she paused beside his bed.

The shock of his voice in the darkness made her freeze. Chance took advantage of her sudden stillness to reach out and tumble her down onto the bed.

5

THE SENSATION OF FALLING was as real emotionally as it was physically. Rachel knew she was losing her balance, in more ways than one, as Chance tugged her down onto the bed. Her head was spinning, and her pulse was racing. She knew what was happening, knew, too, that she should resist. This was madness. It would change everything.

But in that moment, as her mind whirled and her body tumbled lightly across Chance's, Rachel lost her will to resist. The compelling attraction that had been growing between them had finally become undeniable. One look into Chance's gleaming gaze and Rachel knew he'd been aware of the inevitability of the situation long before she had.

She also knew that she'd been drawn to his room tonight by more than the need to check his forehead for fever. She lay sprawled along the length of him, her fingers clutching his shoulders, her robe and gown drifting across the bedclothes. Beneath the fabric of the wool blanket that separated their bodies, Rachel could feel the hard strength of Chance's body.

"I was hoping you'd come back tonight for another look," Chance said. There was a sensual roughness to his gravel-and-ice voice that rifled Rachel's senses. "Last night I nearly went out of my mind when you came in here. But I wasn't in any shape to get you to stay. My head hurt, and my arm was still sore. I knew I'd probably make a hash of it if I tried to make love to you. Tonight things are different."

Rachel caught her breath as she heard the wealth of satisfaction in his voice. She couldn't think of anything else to say except, "You were awake last night when I checked on you?"

"I was awake. And thoroughly frustrated." His hands moved along her sides, gliding warmly down to her hips. "Tonight I was lying here hoping for another chance." He smiled faintly in the shadows. "Tell me you couldn't stay away, Rachel. Tell me you had to come in here. Tell me this is where you want to be tonight."

She shook her head in mute denial. The curving wings of her hair moved gently around her face. "This is the last place I should be tonight."

"You don't mean that," he told her fiercely. He captured her face between two excitingly rough palms, studying her serious, desperate expression. "You know you don't mean that." He pulled her head down to his, kissing her with a drugging urgency.

Rachel moaned and opened her mouth to offer a last protest against fate and her own vulnerability. But the protest was never uttered. Chance was invading her mouth before she could find any words, and his claim overwhelmed the last of her need to struggle against him.

It might be stupid, insane and utterly incomprehensible, but Rachel knew this was what she wanted. She wanted Abraham Chance in a way she had never before in her life wanted anyone or anything. She sighed into his mouth, and her stiffly held body began to melt along the hardness of his.

"That's it, honey," Chance breathed, wrapping his arms around her. "Just relax and stop fighting it. I'll take care of everything."

His words continued as he slowly stripped the robe and nightgown from her trembling body. He talked to her between liquid, then flaming kisses, urging, reassuring, coaxing and compelling her into full surrender. Rachel's head was spinning more than ever now. The soft, dangerous excitement enveloping her was unlike anything she'd ever known. She clutched at Chance, unconsciously using him to steady her reeling emotions.

The last of her garments came free, and Chance slid his hand down to her hip, cupping one soft buttock. He squeezed gently and then laughed a little raggedly when Rachel gasped and buried her face against his shoulder.

"You're going to freeze out there on top of the covers. Come in here where it's warm." He pushed aside the blanket and settled Rachel next to him.

"Chance," she whispered in soft wonder as she felt the heat and hardness of him reaching out for her, "you're so . . . so . . ." Her words trailed off in confusion.

"So ready for you? Is that what you're trying to say? I know. I told you I was lying here waiting and hoping you'd show up again tonight."

"You've been lying here in this condition?" she asked breathlessly. "All this time?"

"Thought I'd go out of my mind." He found her small, curving breast and stroked gently. She trembled in response. "But now I know I'll survive. You feel so good, sweetheart. So good." He leaned over her, covering her mouth once more as he urged her nipple into a firm bud of desire.

She didn't just *want* him tonight, Rachel suddenly realized. She needed him. Her arms went around him as she sought the solid shape and feel of him. It was as though she could learn the truth about him through this most primitive form of communication. In the morning, perhaps, she would see the foolishness in her thinking, but tonight the future seemed very far away. Chance filled her whole world.

Rachel gave herself up to the joy of exploring her lover's lean, hard body. Everything about him fascinated her. She drew her palm down his back, finding the strong, contoured muscles there. He groaned beneath her touch and pulled her closer. The heavy, waiting shaft of his manhood brushed against her thigh, and Rachel flinched.

"It's all right, sweetheart," Chance muttered thickly. "I've told you, everything's going to be all right. Trust me tonight."

"It's not a question of trust," she said awkwardly. She stroked his hip with uncertain fingers. "At least, not exactly."

"What is it, then?" he asked coaxingly as he nuzzled the softness of her throat.

"It's just that there's more of you than I, uh, expected." Embarrassed by the idiocy of her observation, she ducked her head and found her lips on his flat nipple. Instinctively she put out the tip of her tongue and tasted him. Chance sucked in his breath.

"Don't worry about it," he said with a husky chuckle. "Something tells me we're going to fit together beautifully." He moved his palm down over her stomach until his fingers sank into the soft hair below. When one callused fingertip found the small bud that is the focus of feminine sensation, it was Rachel's turn to fight for breath. Deliberately Chance stroked her, holding her even more tightly when she arched in his arms.

"*Chance.*"

"That's it, sweetheart. Come alive for me." He dipped lower, parting the softness of her and finding the sweet, warm dampness he had provoked. When he slipped one finger into her, Rachel shivered and cried out.

Her response inflamed him. She could feel his control fading rapidly, and the knowledge that she had such power over him fed Rachel's own desires. Suddenly she was all woman, sure of her sensual power and glorying in the response she was eliciting in this one particular man. She wanted to please him, entice him, torment him and satisfy him. She reached out to touch him as intimately as he was touching her.

Chance felt the skyrocketing eagerness in her and muttered short, hoarse commands into her ear as he pulled her closer still.

"Touch me," he whispered fiercely. "Yes, like that. I want to feel your fingers all over me. Lower. Yes. *Yes.* Tighter, harder. God, don't be shy with me, sweetheart. Not tonight. I need to know you want me. Again. Do that again, love. Can you feel how much I need you? I'm going to explode inside you. I'm going to go up in flames when I make you mine. I knew from the first you were going to be able to do this to me. I shouldn't have waited this long to make it happen. I was a fool not to drag you off to bed that first night."

She heard the words but she was only half listening to the actual meaning. Most of what impinged on her senses was the tone and feel of them. She heard the masculine need, the sharp, demanding desire, the promise of fulfillment, the urgent command to surrender herself to him completely.

"I want you, Chance. I didn't know . . . I didn't realize how much. I didn't know it would be like this." She urged his mouth down to her breast and sighed when he willingly took her nipple into his mouth. She felt his tongue and then the faint, exciting edge of his teeth. Her fingers tightened in his hair.

The flaring excitement continued to build between them. Safe in the warm darkness under the quilt, they explored each other, murmuring words of promise and passion. Rachel was lost in the mindless world of sensation that Chance had created. She could think of nothing else except the magic of the moment.

Chance never let up the pressure. To Rachel every movement, every stroke, every word seemed expressly designed to stoke the fires within her. She had never known such an explosive sensation. When he moved at last, parting her legs and positioning himself at the very entrance to her secret softness, she wrapped her arms around him.

She closed her eyes, preparing herself for the first, hard thrust she was sure would trigger ecstasy. But for a taut instant he lay tensely still above her, making no attempt to complete the inevitable union.

Rachel lifted her lashes and found him watching her with glittering, smoldering eyes. "What is it, Chance? What's wrong?"

"Sweetheart, you're not thinking clearly tonight and that's just the way I want you, but I've got to know something."

"What?" She stirred beneath him, aware of the weight of him as he crushed her into the bedding.

"Are you using anything?"

She drew a quick breath as she understood his meaning. Then, feeling dazed and foolish, she slowly shook her head. "No. No, I . . . there's no one else. I haven't had any reason to use . . . I mean, I, oh Chance, I'm sorry. This was very stupid of me. I don't know what happened."

"Hush." He bent his head and stopped the flow of confused, apologetic words with a hard, lingering kiss. When he lifted his head again, there was a slight, satisfied smile edging his mouth. "I'm very, very glad there's no one else and that you haven't got any reason to be on the pill or packing a diaphragm. It simplifies life considerably." He started to pull away from her.

Instinctively Rachel clutched at him. "Don't go," she begged, knowing even as she spoke that they couldn't take the risk.

He touched her gently, trailing a fingertip down the side of her cheek to the corner of her mouth. "I'm not going far. Stay right where you are."

He reached across to the bedside table. Rachel heard the drawer being opened, and then she caught the faint sound of a little foil packet being opened. She closed her eyes, half in relief and half in chagrined embarrassment for not having worried about this particular problem much earlier in the course of events.

"It's a good thing one of us is prepared," Chance said with a rough, sexy chuckle as he came back to her, "or we would have been obliged to get very creative tonight." He kissed her again, his hand slipping down between her legs to make certain she was still ready for him.

"When did you . . . ? I . . . I suppose you always have that sort of thing on hand," Rachel mumbled.

He nibbled her ear. "You want the truth? I bought a box yesterday in town while you were getting my prescription filled at the pharmacy."

"Oh." She didn't know what else to say.

"Stop worrying," Chance ordered softly. "I told you I'd take care of everything. Now put your arms around me and tell me you want me."

She obeyed, smiling tremulously. "I want you. What happens next?" she asked.

He grinned with devilish sensuality. "This is your lucky night. You're going to get what you want."

He started to guide himself into her, and the wicked grin vanished as he felt the convulsive way her body clenched around him. His eyes burned as he looked down into her face. "You're so warm," he gasped. "So small. You feel so damn good." He surged forward, filling her completely.

Rachel cried out as his body invaded hers. For an instant she thought it wasn't going to work, in spite of Chance's assurances. And then he was deep inside, stroking slowly and deliberately as her body adjusted to his. His hands tightened on her shoulders, and his mouth drank the soft sighs from her lips.

When she began to respond, Chance groaned, the muscles of his hips tightening beneath her hands. "That's it," he whispered. "So good. So good. Just right." He inserted one hand between their bodies and found the small nub hidden in the curls between her legs. And all the while he kept up the slow, careful stroking rhythm.

Rachel thought she was going to come apart and shatter into a thousand crystal pieces. A swirling excitement was rippling through her, teaching her new secrets about her body and its ability to respond. She clutched at Chance, pleading with him for an answer to a question she wasn't quite sure how to ask.

But he knew what she wanted. When her hips lifted frantically against his and her body began to tense in unbearable desire, he moved deeply into her.

"Now," he muttered. "Let it go now."

She obeyed, her nerve endings convulsing in a final, blazing response to the delightful, sensual torture they had been enduring.

"Chance, oh, please, Chance, I can't stand it."

"Do you think I can?"

And then he was joining her as she went over the edge. His hoarse shout filled the small room, mingling with her soft cries of release.

Rachel felt herself drifting downward, held fast in Chance's arms as the sparkling remnants of satisfaction slowly dissolved and disappeared. She closed her eyes, not wanting to face the fact that this very special interlude was over. Morning would come soon enough. She didn't have to start worrying about it tonight.

Chance kissed her lazily as he carefully lifted himself away from her. "Are you going to be a female chauvinist and just roll over and go to sleep now that you've had your wicked way with me?"

She stirred. "I'm sorry."

He cradled her. "Don't be. To tell you the truth, I'm more exhausted than you are. I'm still recovering from grievous wounds, remember?"

Instantly her lashes lifted in startled concern. "Chance, are you all right? How are you feeling?"

"What a question." He touched the tip of her nose. "I'm feeling fantastic." He smiled with knowing satisfaction. "How about you?"

She bit her lip. "I think you already know the answer to that."

"Maybe I just want to hear the words," he said seriously.

She searched his face. "Why?"

"Because then I can tell myself I'm making progress on one problem, at least."

"What problem?" she demanded uneasily.

"The problem of getting you to trust me."

"Is that what you want?" she asked quietly.

"It would be reassuring to hear you say the words. You're such a wary little thing, always watching me as if you're wondering how far to trust me. Now that you've trusted me this far, I'd like to hear you admit it."

"You think making love with you automatically means I've decided to trust you?"

"I hope it does."

She fumbled with the covers, sitting up and reaching for her nightgown, which was lying at the foot of the bed. "I don't know what you're talking about, Chance. You're a terrific lover and, after what just happened, I'm sure you know it. It's very late. I'd better get back to my room."

"Hey, where do you think you're going?" He caught her hand and snapped the nightgown from her grasp.

"Back to my room."

"No, you're not. You're staying here tonight." He tugged her back down beside him. "Okay, so you're not the type to get chatty after sex. I'm adaptable. I'm willing to wait until morning to talk."

"Talk about what? Chance, you're not making any sense." Rachel began to panic. Maybe he knew something was wrong. He had to suspect something, or he wouldn't have made that comment about talking in the morning. He was trying to coax her into confessing everything. And heaven help her, if she weren't very careful she was liable to blurt out the whole truth about just why she was here at Snowball's Chance. The worst of it was she wanted to tell him. She wanted to get it all into the open and hear his side of the story.

"Chance, I . . ."

"Take it easy," he murmured, pulling her back down into the circle of his arms. "What does it take to make you understand that you don't have to fly into a panic every time I get close? When are you going to really trust me, sweetheart?"

She couldn't find the words to answer him. Instead she turned her face into his chest and clung to him while he held her and stroked her. Frantically she sought for some flippant, throwaway remark that might lessen the tension.

"I'm sorry," she finally whispered against his skin. "I'm not used to sleeping with my employers."

"No," he said thoughtfully, "I can see that. Go to sleep, honey. We'll hash this out in the morning."

RACHEL CAME AWAKE SLOWLY the next morning, deliberately allowing herself to adjust to the watery sunshine and the feel of a man's hard, muscular body next to hers. She stayed very still for a long moment until she was certain Chance wasn't awake. Then she began to ease out of bed.

Her foot was just touching the cold floor when a male hand snaked out from under the covers and clamped around her wrist.

"Am I going to have to chain you down to keep you from running off every time you think I'm not looking?" Chance asked without opening his eyes.

She tensed, her own eyes coming around quickly to stare at his stark face. His dark hair was invitingly ruffled, and his bronzed skin was a sexy contrast to the snowy whiteness of the pillow. The sheet and blankets were bunched around his waist, and she could see the crisp curls on his sleekly muscled chest.

"I didn't know you were awake. You need your sleep, Chance. I was just going to take a shower."

"You're a lousy liar, do you know that? A very sweet liar, but not a very accomplished one." He opened his eyes. The smoke of his gaze settled on her, bringing a warm flush to her face.

Rachel felt cornered. She took the only way out by going on the defensive. "Are you very good at detecting liars, Chance?"

"I've had my share of experience."

"Are you always right?" she challenged, thinking of her stepsister.

"Let's just say I'm usually right. Nobody's perfect."

He was right about that, Rachel thought. He had been less than perfect when he'd "solved" the case in which Gail had been involved. But maybe he didn't realize just how wrong he'd been. "What would you do if you discovered you'd been wrong about . . . about something very important, Chance?"

He watched her coolly. "Generally speaking, I'd do whatever I could to fix things."

"Would you?" She held her breath. Maybe, just maybe there was a way out of this mess. Against her will she had developed a certain respect for this man. He didn't seem the type to throw an innocent victim to the wolves for the sake of his reputation as an investigator. Maybe, if he knew her side of the story, heard her theories on what had happened at her sister's firm, he would be willing to reopen the case.

Or maybe she was clutching at straws because she'd fallen in love with him.

Rachel made her decision. She had no choice, because she knew now she could never carry out a suitable vengeance. She had proved that to herself last night when she'd made love with Abraham Chance.

"Chance," she began earnestly, "I want to talk to you. There's something important I want to say."

He smiled slowly, his expression very satisfied. "It's about time."

Rachel started to plunge ahead, but something stopped her. She didn't like that look of satisfaction. It reminded her that she was dealing with a man who made his living unmasking liars and thieves and other assorted villains. He looked as if he were about to unmask another one right now.

And Gail had claimed Chance had seduced her in order to frame her.

A chilling thought struck Rachel. She had to face the possibility that Chance had deliberately seduced her last night just to get some answers to the questions he apparently had about her.

Uncertainty clouded her mind. She needed time to think. Rachel reached down to scoop her robe up off the floor. "I want to shower and dress first," she mumbled.

He released her with obvious reluctance. "All right, little coward. Have it your way. But don't spend too long in the bathroom, or I might decide to see if there's room for two in that old shower stall."

"There's not," she assured him, bolting for the door.

Just to be on the safe side, Rachel didn't delay in the bathroom.

Twenty minutes later she was busy fixing breakfast and listening for the assorted thumps from upstairs that would tell her Chance was finished with his shower. She wasn't looking forward to his arrival downstairs. He would be hungry for answers as well as pancakes.

Now there was no doubt in her mind that he knew she had secrets. When she looked back over the past few days, she realized he had deliberately given her a variety of opportunities to confide in him. Last night he had delivered his coup de grace. He must be congratulating himself right this moment, thinking he'd broken through her barriers. He would be expecting a full explanation for her presence at Snowball's Chance.

But if she could persuade him to reassess his conclusions about her stepsister, it might all be worth it, Rachel thought as she braced herself for the coming ordeal. Chance seemed a basically honest man. There was an unmistakable integrity about him that simply didn't fit with the image she'd been given by Gail.

Rachel was almost certain she would be able to convince Chance to at least listen to her side of the incident.

She sliced open a cantaloupe while she tried to make up her mind about how to tell Chance the truth. She would have to approach the matter with care. Chance wasn't going to be thrilled to find out who she was, even if he could be persuaded to help her.

It was then that Rachel heard the sound of a car in the drive.

She looked out the kitchen window and saw a young woman climbing out of a small sports car. The stranger was fair and blond and very attractive. Also very young, probably about twenty or so. She was wearing expensive-looking trousers and a silk shirt. Her shining hair was cut in a short, stylish mode, and she had obviously taken the time to put on all her eye makeup before making the drive to Snowball's Chance.

So much for worrying about how to handle the big true-confession scene with Chance this morning, Rachel thought as she put down the knife and went to the front door. It was obvious Chance was going to have other things to do today besides listen to an impassioned plea for justice.

A small, imperious fist pounded on the heavy old door just as Rachel put her hand on the knob. When she opened the door she summoned what she hoped was a proper housekeeper's smile of greeting.

"Good morning," Rachel said politely. "Can I help you?"

The young woman stared at her. "Who in the world are you?"

"I'm Rachel Wilder, Mr. Chance's housekeeper."

"His housekeeper! Since when did he...?" The young woman broke off as she caught sight of Chance coming down the hall stairs. "Chance! There you are. I was praying you were here. I've got to talk to you. You have to listen to me this time."

"I always listen to you, Mindy," Chance said dryly as he reached the door. "I don't always do what you want, but I do listen to you. Rachel, meet my sister, Mindy. When she's not being a pain in the neck or indulging in a fit of melodramatic hysterics or whining piteously, she's actually a rather decent kid. Of course, it's hard to find times when she's not involved in one of her emotional extremes."

"How do you do," Rachel murmured. She held out a hand, but it was ignored. Melinda Chance obviously had other things on her mind than being polite to Chance's housekeeper. She whirled on Chance, her lovely eyes glistening with tears.

Rachel noticed the tears didn't spill over and ruin the artfully applied cosmetics. It occurred to her that Mindy and Gail had something in common. They had both mastered the art of crying without ruining their makeup.

"Chance, I must talk to you in private. My whole life is hanging in the balance. You have to let me have my money. I'm going to get married. I mean it, Chance. This time I really mean it. I love Roarke." There was a dramatic pause. "And I have to marry him."

"Roarke? What happened to Carl?" Chance asked blandly. He glanced at Rachel over his sister's head.

Rachel saw the promise in his gaze and knew that her own very private conversation with him had merely been postponed, not forgotten. Slowly she closed the door as Mindy threw herself into her brother's arms.

"Don't tease me, Chance. This time I have to get married. Don't you understand? I'm . . . *I'm pregnant*."

Rachel caught her breath. "Excuse me," she managed. "This sounds like a, uh, family matter. I'll be in the kitchen."

"That's where I'm headed, too," Chance said easily as he disengaged himself from his sister's grasp. "I haven't had breakfast yet."

"Breakfast!" Mindy yelped plaintively. "How can you think about breakfast at a time like this?"

Chance glanced at his watch. "It's the perfect time to think about breakfast. It's nearly eight o'clock. Actually, it's a little late, if you want to get precise about it. Rachel and I slept in this morning. Come to think of it, you're not usually up and around at this hour, Mindy. How far did you drive this morning? All the way from San Francisco?"

"I stayed in a motel a few miles down the road last night," Mindy said, brushing aside the insignificant question. "Chance, I—"

"Excuse me. I need a cup of Rachel's coffee."

Rachel fled toward the kitchen, but Mindy's desperate voice followed her. "Chance, listen to me. Didn't you hear what I said? I'm pregnant. I have to marry Roarke. This time I have no choice."

"Well, I certainly wish you the best of luck," Chance said cheerfully as he ambled into the kitchen and sat down. "What does this Roarke do for a living? Is he going to be able to support a wife and a kid? Have you warned him you're addicted to charge cards?"

"He's a writer," Mindy declared proudly as she hurried after her brother. "You can't expect him to work. You'll have to let me have access to my money, Chance. Roarke and I . . . and the baby will need it in order to survive."

"Babies don't eat much, do they, Rachel? A little milk, a little mush. That's all. Shouldn't cost a lot. I doubt you'll need to dip into your capital. How about it, Rachel? Had any experience with babies?"

Rachel shot him a quick glance, horrified to find herself being drawn into the conversation. "I'm afraid I don't know anything about them," she mumbled as she hastily poured pancake batter onto the old iron griddle. "I've never had a baby." Lord, what an idiotic thing to say. She remembered the moment when Chance had called a brief halt to their lovemaking last night so he could take care of the precautions. She felt herself turning red.

"Chance, this is between you and me. I'm sure Rachel doesn't want to hear about my situation," Mindy hissed.

"I'm sure housekeepers are accustomed to the facts of life," Chance said casually as he poured the coffee. "They must get exposed to them all the time. Probably goes with the territory, right, Rachel?"

Rachel turned redder as she realized he was teasing her about last night. "Would you like some pancakes, Mindy?" she asked desperately.

"I couldn't eat a thing," Mindy said flatly. She turned back to Chance. "I'm not leaving here until you agree to turn loose my money, Chance, do you understand me? I am going to marry Roarke."

"You can stay for a day or two as long as you don't make a nuisance of yourself," Chance informed her as he accepted a plate of pancakes from Rachel. "Knowing you, though, Mindy, you will make a nuisance of yourself. You're already becoming very irritating. You know I can't stand whining first thing in the morning. I figure by tomorrow you'll have developed into a full-blown nuisance. Either that or you'll get tired of helping out around here."

"Helping out! I didn't come here to help out," Mindy said pathetically, her eyes turning a damper shade of blue. "I came to talk to you about my forthcoming marriage."

"If you stay here, you'll have to make yourself useful. Rachel could use a hand around the house. There's a lot to be done."

"Chance, haven't you been listening? I'm going to get married!"

"Please, don't bring up the subject again during breakfast. And please don't cry. I have a delicate stomach." Chance picked up his fork and dug into Rachel's pancakes with a gusto that belied his claim.

Rachel stood next to the stove, watching him eat and studying the desperate-looking young woman sitting across from him. Rachel found herself wondering how she would react if Gail had just announced she was pregnant and had to get married.

Rachel knew she would never have been able to adopt Chance's casual attitude toward the whole matter. In fact, his attitude appalled her. This was his sister who was sitting here pleading for help and understanding. His young, pregnant, unwed sister. Didn't the man have any sympathy or compassion at all?

Chance was proving himself every bit as callous and unfeeling as she had once thought him. It shocked her to realize she had actually come close to telling him the full truth about herself that morning. She had actually been convinced that she'd be able to talk him into helping her prove her sister innocent. No, he was hardly likely to help her.

Rachel stared at Chance wolfing down pancakes and knew that Mindy's arrival had saved her from making a drastic mistake.

6

THE CONFUSION Rachel had been feeling since Melinda Chance had appeared at the door metamorphosed into a seething anger as breakfast progressed. While Rachel listened to Melinda's desperate pleading and Chance's heartless responses she came to the only logical conclusion. A man who wouldn't go out of his way to help his pregnant sister was hardly likely to help the sister of a woman with whom he'd shared a single night in bed.

Rachel decided she had to get away from Snowball's Chance.

She had come very close to making the biggest mistake of her life by confiding everything to Chance. He clearly had no doubts at all about his own conclusions in any given situation. Nor did he allow sentiment to sway him. As far as he was concerned he was right, and everyone else could damn well pick up the pieces.

Rachel had been indulging in wishful thinking brought on by a night of sensual illusion. Chance had nearly seduced her into telling him everything. He suspected something was wrong where his housekeeper was concerned, and his curiosity was aroused. That was all.

Well, not quite all, Rachel thought bitterly. She remembered the power and intensity of his lovemaking and winced.

She told herself she had to leave as quickly as possible, and she made up her mind to use excuses similar to those of the vanished Mrs. Vinson. A difficult job and an impossible employer. Rachel's mouth curved grimly as she decided Chance would undoubtedly understand. If she got away immediately, he might be left with some questions about the odd housekeeper who had dropped into his life and then disappeared. But he wouldn't have any answers. He couldn't track her down even if he wanted to.

At least, she didn't think he could. Rachel frowned thoughtfully.

She was clearing the table when Chance finished the last of his pancakes and coffee, pushed back his chair and got to his feet. He threw a disgusted glance at his sister and a grim one at Rachel. It was clear his initial derisive humor was almost gone. As his sister's impassioned, tearful pleas had continued, his mood had become one of irritated impatience.

"Breakfast is over. I'm going out to the coach house. I've got better things to do than sit here arguing all morning. Rachel, I want to talk to you later in private."

"Yes, sir." Rachel inclined her head in what she knew was a mockery of a housekeeper's deference. Chance glowered at her but apparently decided not to pursue the matter in front of his sister.

"As for you, Mindy, you're welcome to stay only if you can manage to make yourself reasonably pleasant and helpful. I told you earlier, I haven't got time to entertain idle guests. If you stick around you'll have to pitch in and give Rachel a hand inside the house. There's a lot to be done."

"Chance, I came here to talk to you," Melinda said frantically.

"We've been over this particular topic one too many times. I've given you my answer one too many times. You're not getting your hands on that money. Not until you've learned to handle your life like the adult you're supposed to be. Now, either you change the subject or you go back to San Francisco. If you stay here I don't want to hear another word about your forthcoming marriage."

"But the baby..."

"I don't want to hear about it, either."

"Damn it, Chance, you haven't even met Roarke. How can you be so brutal about this? My whole future is at stake."

"One more word on the subject, Mindy, and you can hop back in your car and leave. Clear?"

"But, Chance, please..."

Chance didn't raise his voice, but the gravel and ice of his words were suddenly sharp, cold stones. "I asked if we have a clear understanding. Because if we don't, I'll expect you to be gone by lunch. This is my home, and I'm not about to have another meal ruined because of a whimpering, sulking female. Go give the soon-to-be-famous Roarke a sample of your tantrums. If he's going to marry you, he'd better learn to cope with them."

Melinda bit her lip and turned away, tears glistening once more in her beautiful eyes. Her head ducked in what might have been taken for an affirmative response. Chance took it that way and stalked out of the house. A moment later the door slammed behind him.

Rachel stood at the sink, a dishrag in her hand, and wondered what to do next. The last thing she needed was to get involved in the quarrel between Chance and his sister. But it was difficult not to feel sympathy for Melinda, who sat looking very forlorn and lost at the kitchen table. She had seen Gail look just like that at various times in the past.

"Excuse me," Rachel said gently as she removed the last of the dishes. "Would you like some coffee?"

Melinda looked up at her as if surprised to find someone else in the room. She had hardly noticed Rachel's presence until now. Her whole attention had been given to the impassioned argument with her brother.

"Are you really Chance's housekeeper?" Melinda asked unexpectedly.

Rachel's eyebrows rose slightly. "If you'd seen how the place looked a few days ago when I arrived and compared it to how it looks now, you wouldn't ask that."

Melinda glanced around, as if to assess how much work had been done. "It's just that you don't look like a housekeeper. When you answered the door this morning I assumed you were here to, uh, entertain my brother."

Rachel hoped the flush on her cheeks was hidden as she turned smoothly back to the sink. "Your brother is too busy getting Snowball's Chance in shape to use it as a love nest," she pointed out tartly. "Any woman who hangs around here is going to be put to work, and I don't mean in bed."

Melinda sighed. "He's really fixated on this place, isn't he? Lord knows what he sees in the dump. If he had any sense he'd sell it. Forget what I said about playing geisha. I know Chance well enough to realize that once he's got a project he's single-minded about it until it's completed. Right now fixing up Snowball's Chance is his big goal. He's been talking about it ever since Dad died and left it to him. Now that he's finally got the time and some money to do the job, the last thing he's liable to do is invite a woman up here to play bedroom games." Melinda paused and then added angrily, "Not unless he could get her to agree to play housekeeper, too, and frankly I don't know of many women who would fall for that package arrangement."

Rachel cleared her throat, not certain how to respond. "Is that right?"

"Sure. Just ask one who knows him well. There are plenty of women willing to have an affair with him but very few who would actually work for him. He's a real slave driver. His secretaries at Dixon Security were always quitting on him. He's blunt and ruthless and totally lacking in finesse." Melinda picked up the cup of coffee Rachel set in front of her. "Most of his affairs haven't lasted very long, either, come to think of it. Chance is not a kind man."

Not a kind man. Rachel's mouth tightened. To think she'd been about to confess all to him and ask for help. Chance would probably have bitten her head off before kicking her out of Snowball's Chance.

Let that be a lesson to you, my girl, she told herself fiercely. *Just because a man is tender and loving in bed does not mean he'll be kind and gentle out of it.* A man did what he had to do in order to get the response he wanted from a woman. Once he had that response, he reverted to his true self.

"Rachel, I don't know what I'm going to do," Melinda went on in tones of utter despair. "I love Roarke, and he loves me. But we need my money for the first few years. Just until Roarke gets published and established in the literary world. It won't take long. He's brilliant, really he is. I just know he's going to write the bestselling novel of the decade. But a writer has to be able to devote himself to his craft."

"That's a luxury most writers probably can't afford in the beginning," Rachel said quietly. "But it doesn't seem to stop them. In any event, Roarke has you and the baby to worry about as well as his writing. There are such things as priorities."

"It's not fair," Melinda shot back furiously. "It would be different if I had no money of my own, but I do. Dad left all the money to Mother and me. He wanted to make sure we were taken care of. He said Chance could take care of himself. If only he hadn't put Chance in charge of the trust funds. Dad should have guessed what would happen."

"What did happen?"

Melinda looked up at her with brimming eyes. "Chance is probably manipulating the accounts for himself, naturally. Oh, he can't mess with the principal, but he has a lot of leeway to play games with the interest."

"What?" Rachel was truly shocked at that. She could envision Chance being tighter than a fist with the money, but she couldn't see him taking advantage of the funds for his own purposes. "Are you sure of that, Mindy? That's a very strong accusation."

"How do I know what he's doing with the money?" Melinda cried. "All I know is that I never see very much of it. He could be siphoning it off into Swiss bank accounts in his own name for all I know."

Rachel stared thoughtfully at the beautiful blond head bent over the coffee cup. There was no doubt about it, Melinda and Gail both had a streak of the dramatic. Chance might be as hard as a rock in some ways, but now she knew instinctively that he was no thief. "I think you can stop worrying about Chance using your money for his own purposes. He's not the type."

"Well, what type is he, then? What type of man would withhold what's rightfully mine when I'm going to need it to marry and take care of my baby?" Melinda wailed.

Rachel sighed. "A very hard man."

"See? I told you so."

"I said a hard man, Mindy, not an unscrupulous one. There's a difference."

"I don't see the distinction," Melinda said, pulling a hankie out of her purse. "Oh, God, Rachel, what am I going to do about the baby?"

"Chance is not going to stand by and see you and your baby starve," Rachel declared forcefully.

"He's not going to stand by and let me marry Roarke, either, is he?" Melinda sniffed into the hankie. "I'll wind up being an unwed mother. All alone in the world. Just another statistic."

This was not her problem, Rachel decided. She had enough of a disaster on her hands with her own stepsister. It was time to cut her losses and get away from Snowball's Chance.

She finished the last of the dishes and glanced around the kitchen. For some irrational reason she wanted to leave things in good condition. Chance would have a lot to say when he found her gone this afternoon, but she would make very sure he couldn't fault the work she'd done.

"Help yourself to the rest of the coffee," Rachel said as she untied her apron. "I've got some things to do upstairs."

Melinda sniffed again, delicately wiped her nose and reached for the coffee. "Thanks. I could use it. I don't know what I'm going to do now. I guess there's no point in staying here."

Rachel gave the other woman a sympathetic glance and then hurried out the door. She didn't know what Melinda was going to do, either, but she knew what she had to do.

Pack.

Safe in the small, bare room where she'd been sleeping until last night, Rachel began folding the few clothes she'd brought with her and the assorted items she'd picked up in town. The process didn't take long. She was stuffing the last of her makeup into a small, plastic-lined bag when the bedroom door was abruptly slammed open.

"And just where the hell do you think you're going?" Chance asked ominously from the doorway.

Rachel's hands stilled momentarily, but she didn't bother to glance at him. There was no point. She knew what she would see, and it would be intimidating to say the least. "Home," she said succinctly, and went back to pushing makeup into the bag.

"I had a feeling you were up to something. You've been giving me the kind of looks a rabbit gives a snake all morning. But I've got news for you, you're not going anywhere," Chance informed her with lethal calmness as he walked into the room and closed the door very softly behind him.

Rachel went on with her packing. "I'm quitting, Chance. You'll have to find yourself another housekeeper."

"Is that right?" He folded his arms and leaned against the wall. Smoky eyes flicked over her as if she were a relatively unimportant piece of furniture that had just spoken out loud. "And just where am I supposed to find another housekeeper?"

"From the same place you found the first two, I suppose," she retorted without stopping to think.

"That's going to be a little difficult, isn't it? Granted, I know where Mrs. Vinson came from, but I don't know nearly as much about you."

Rachel caught her breath and threw him a startled glance. "I don't understand," she whispered. "You said you knew I was from the same firm that sent Mrs. Vinson."

"That was my initial assumption, but it was wrong, wasn't it? I knew that much within hours after your arrival. I double-checked with the agency. They confirmed they hadn't sent a replacement for Vinson."

She stared at him. He had known about her almost from the beginning. It was frighteningly unnerving to realize he'd been playing games with her. All the more reason to get out of here. "I see. Well, I hope you have better luck next time. It's tough to get good help these days, isn't it?"

He ignored the flippancy. "There isn't going to be a next time. I don't know how you found out about this position. Maybe from Mrs. Vinson herself. I don't really care. All I do know is that you took the job, and I'm tired of changing housekeepers. It's as bad as changing secretaries. You're staying, lady."

"Not a chance. I'm leaving for all the same reasons Mrs. Vinson left—and then some." At least he still assumed she was some sort of housekeeper, even if she wasn't from the agency he'd been dealing with. That was something. Rachel didn't want this man asking too many questions about her after she left. She tossed the makeup bag into her small suitcase and started to slam the lid.

Chance moved, coming away from the wall with a speed that took Rachel completely by surprise. He caught the suitcase lid before she could get it completely closed. He flung it open again. "It's because of last night, isn't it? Or at least that's what you're telling yourself."

"Last night was a mistake," she said tightly. He was too close. Deliberately she edged away from him. But she was forced to halt when he put a hand behind her neck and anchored her in place. Rachel lifted resentful eyes to his implacable gaze. "I'm leaving, Chance."

"If you do, you'd better be prepared for me to follow. Because I'll be right on your heels, Rachel."

The cold promise in his words shocked her. Her eyes widened. "You'd follow me? You can't do that."

He smiled grimly at her naiveté. "Want to bet?"

"You *can't*."

"I will, I swear it. You're not getting away from me. Not until you've answered all the questions I've got about you."

"Questions! I'm not about to answer any questions. What questions could you have about me, anyway?"

she hissed. "I'm just a housekeeper you decided to turn into a bedroom convenience." She tried to free herself from his grasp and failed.

His eyes glittered. "Just for the record, let's get one thing clear. You're the one who came to my room last night. I did not go to yours."

"I only went in to check you for fever!"

"And you found out I was running one, didn't you? It's true, Rachel. I seem to have developed a fever for you. I'm not sure how or why you came into my life, but you're here now, and you're going to stay until this fever of mine has run its course. Try to leave, and I'll chase you down and bring you back. Don't tell yourself I couldn't find you if I tried. It's my business to be able to find people when they don't want to be found."

"Don't you dare threaten me!"

"Why not? I'll try anything it takes to keep you where I want you until I know all there is to know about you."

"There's nothing to know about me," she said helplessly. "Except that I don't sleep with my employers."

"Is that the real reason you're trying to run away this morning?" he challenged softly.

"Do I need any other reason?"

"Yes, damn it, you do. That one's just not good enough. What's more, I'm not buying it."

Fury overwhelmed her. "Is that right? If you want another excuse, I'll give you one. I don't happen to like working for a man who treats his sister the way you do. You were callous, brutal and totally unfeeling this morning when poor Mindy showed up on your doorstep. It makes me think you're probably inclined to be callous, brutal and unfeeling about other women in your life, too. That's not an encouraging thought. I have no interest in being a . . . a mistress and a house-keeper for a man who has no heart!"

Chance's other hand came up to grip her shoulder. He gave her a slight shake, just enough to convey a small measure of his simmering annoyance. "You're in no position to judge me, Rachel Wilder. You know very little about the situation between me and my sister, so don't jump to any conclusions."

"I'm not jumping to conclusions. I'm merely making some informed decisions based on what I observed with my own eyes this morning," she said through set teeth. "You were totally uncaring in response to a situation that requires a great deal of compassion and care and tact."

"I should be compassionate and caring and tactful toward a spoiled, manipulative little girl who took one too many drama classes in high school? I should turn a large sum of money over to a woman who would run through it in a year or eighteen months with the help of her latest boyfriend, the great American novelist? Mindy is not yet sufficiently grown-up to be trusted with next month's rent, let alone a good-sized trust fund."

"But she's going to need some of it," Rachel said. "After all, she's pregnant. And if this Roarke person doesn't have a job—"

Chance raised his eyes briefly toward heaven. "Give me a break, Rachel. Mindy is no more pregnant than I am."

Rachel was dumbfounded. "What in the world are you talking about?"

"You heard me. Take my word for it, Mindy is not pregnant. She may be spoiled, manipulative and overly dramatic, and she has a bad habit of whining when she can't get her own way, but she's not completely stupid. She has no desire to be saddled with a kid at her age. She's got too many plans and, believe me, right now none of them involves playing Mommy."

Rachel stared at him. "But she said she was pregnant. That's why she wants to get married."

Chance shook his head. "She's lying," he said simply.

"Lying?"

"Well, she probably thinks of it as a small fib told in a good cause, but as far as I'm concerned, it's a lie. Christ, don't tell me you were taken in by that sniffling little scene down in the kitchen?"

"How can you be so sure she's not telling the truth about the baby?" Rachel demanded in a stifled voice.

Chance shrugged. "Believe me, I know. I've had to deal with Mindy since the day she was born. I've got her figured out from the word go. But even if I didn't know her all that well, I'd still be fairly certain the bit about the baby was pure fiction."

His obvious belief in the infallibility of his own conclusions enraged Rachel. "How could you possibly be
certain without a note from her doctor?"

"Instinct."

"What instinct? Some grand male instinct that automatically assumes all women are liars when they're
under pressure."

His sudden grin further infuriated her. "Actually,
that's not an altogether false assumption. The truth is,
anyone will lie if the pressure is great enough. Survival
mechanism, I suppose. But not very many people can
do it very well. At least, I've never had much trouble
telling the lies from the various and assorted shades of
truth. Besides, I've got some more evidence against
Mindy. When I came through the kitchen just now she
told me she hadn't yet informed Roarke or Beth of this
famous pregnancy. She asked me to keep quiet about it
while she plans her future. Translated, that means she
can't back up the pregnancy story and therefore doesn't
want it spread around."

"You're so blasted sure of yourself, aren't you?"

"Before this is all over," he said quietly, "I intend to
be sure of you. Now unpack your suitcase and get to
work. Find something for Mindy to do, too. It shouldn't
be hard. Who knows? With any luck she'll take one
look at a scrub brush and head for San Francisco."

"You're trying to get rid of her?"

"Damn right. I don't particularly want her hanging
around. She's a nuisance, especially when there's work
to be done. Besides, she never did like this place."

Rachel drew herself up, and her eyes blazed with her emotions as she faced him. "As it happens, I don't particularly like Snowball's Chance, either."

"You'll get used to it," he told her carelessly. "The place grows on you."

"Like a fungus?"

"Like a headstrong, gutsy, recalcitrant but very sexy female who turns all soft and loving when the lights go out." He leaned down and kissed her forehead before she could move. "Now get busy. I'm not paying for standing-around time."

"You're not paying for *any* of my time. I'm not staying here, Chance," Rachel sputtered.

He released her and walked to the door. He paused with one hand on the old glass knob, turned and looked at her over his shoulder. There was a cool, sardonic expression in his eyes that was nothing short of intimidating. Rachel chewed nervously on her lower lip even as she tried to face him squarely. Instantly the smoky gaze went to her mouth. Chance nodded once.

"You'll stay until I tell you that you can go." He opened the door. "Because if you put me to the trouble of coming after you, Rachel, I can promise you I won't be in a kind or generous mood. Believe it." He strode out into the hall without waiting for a response.

Rachel stood by the bed, the open suitcase beside her. *Not a kind man.* "I believe you," she heard herself say. She sank down on the edge of the bed. "Heaven help me, I believe you."

She sat staring at the bare wooden floor, trying to think clearly. It was difficult. She felt as if her emotions had been put through a wringer since she'd arrived at Snowball's Chance. A fulminating need for revenge had been twisted into a crazy wish to ask Chance for his help, thanks to her own stupidity and a burning sensuality that had blindsided her.

The truth had arrived in the shape of one Melinda Chance, and Rachel felt as if she'd been sandbagged by reality. Her fierce desire to escape the mounting pressure had been confronted with the inescapable threat of Chance's pursuing her.

He would do it, too. She knew that with a frightening certainty. She no longer tried to convince herself she could hide from him. And if he came after her, he would learn the full truth about her. He would know that she'd tried to play a very dangerous game of revenge with him at Snowball's Chance, and he would be furious.

Not a kind man. Not a man who would let secrets go unresolved.

But she couldn't simply stay here and wait out the storm. She couldn't assume he would grow tired of trying to probe beneath the surface of her housekeeper image. Chance knew she had secrets. He wanted answers, and if she stuck around she knew that sooner or later he would get them. Yet giving him answers would serve no useful purpose. He would never admit he might have been wrong about Gail.

No, the only thing that would happen now if Rachel told Chance the truth would be a unpleasant confrontation with his temper. She remembered telling Keith Braxton that she was quite certain Chance possessed a very lethal temper. She didn't want to face it.

She was sure Abraham Chance would be far more ruthless and thorough in his revenge than she'd ever dreamed of being in hers.

She felt trapped.

Rachel got to her feet, reminding herself that Chance didn't really know who she was. He had a name and a description, but that was about all he had at this stage. The thing to do was to let the situation cool down a little before she made her move.

Perhaps when he realized she had no intention of playing mistress as well as housekeeper he would lose interest in her secrets. If he lost interest in her, he wouldn't bother to come after her when she left.

Or perhaps she was fooling herself.

Rachel went downstairs and picked up the keys to the Toyota. Melinda was no longer sitting at the kitchen table. She had probably gone to the coach house to plead her cause with Chance.

Rachel stepped out onto the front porch and closed the door behind her. She was halfway to the Toyota when Chance materialized behind her.

"Going somewhere?" he asked casually.

She swung around and saw him leaning on a rake, his dark hair ruffled, his denim shirt unbuttoned halfway down his chest. Rachel lifted her chin and tossed her keys into the air. "Into town to get more food for dinner. I haven't got enough on hand for three. There are a few other things I need, also." She caught the keys in her fingers, and her hand tightened around them. The metal teeth bit into her soft palm.

Chance studied her for a long moment and then nodded. He picked up the rake. "Don't be gone long. And try to buy efficiently this time. Every trip into town is at least an hour away from your job."

"Yes, sir," she retorted smartly, and wrenched open the door of the Toyota. When she was safely inside the vehicle she rolled down the window and gave him a glance that contained all her brooding defiance. "Mrs. Vinson was right, you know. You are arrogant, rude and impossible to work for."

"Too bad you need this job so badly, huh?"

She did not dignify that with a response. Twisting the keys in the ignition, she swung the wheel of the Toyota and shot off down the road to the temporary freedom of town.

Chance watched the car until it was out of sight, and then he turned and walked toward the house. He was halfway there when Melinda appeared from the coach house.

"Chance? Where are you going? I'm not through talking to you yet."

"I'm through talking to you, though, Mindy. That makes all the difference." He kept going toward the front door, ignoring his sister's angrily stomped foot.

"I just want you to agree to meet Roarke. Is that too much to ask?" she wailed behind him.

"Probably. At the moment I've got something else to take care of." He hesitated and turned back briefly. "By the way, I've changed my mind about letting you stay. There's no way you're going to make yourself useful, so you might as well get out. Run along back to San Francisco. Say hello to Mom for me." He let the tattered screen door slam shut.

Chance went into the hall and picked up the phone. He dialed a familiar number and waited impatiently until a secretary's polite voice answered.

"Dixon Security."

"Get me Dixon."

"I'm sorry, sir, Mr. Dixon is in conference at the moment. Can I take a message?"

"Who the hell is this?"

"I'm Sandra, sir. And I'll be glad to help you in any way I can, but Mr. Dixon is simply unavailable at the moment."

Chance sighed. "You must be new there, Sandra."

"I just started this week, sir."

"Then you have a lot to learn. You might as well start now. Tell Dixon that Chance is on the phone."

"But, sir . . ."

"Do it."

There was a discreet pause. When Sandra spoke again her voice had turned aloof and chilly. "Just a moment, sir."

Dixon was on the line a minute later. "Chance? It's about time you called. Finally came to your senses, huh? I knew you would, boy. I knew you wouldn't let our little disagreement over what happened at Truett & Tully Electronics ruin a great working relationship. Come on back, Chance. Your office is still empty and waiting for you. I'll even get you a new secretary, one who hasn't had a chance to hear about your reputation. How about Sandra?"

"Forget it, Herb, I'm not calling to tell you I've changed my mind. I'm calling because you owe me a few favors. I'm going to collect one today."

Dixon groaned. "I was afraid of that. I've never known you to change your mind once you've made it up. What is it you want?"

"Information. Anything and everything you can get me about a Miss Rachel Wilder. Got a pen? I'll give you her address." He rattled off the address he had memorized when he'd taken a quick glance at the registration certificate in the Toyota.

"Chance, what is this? Why the sudden interest in somebody named Wilder? Look, you and I should talk. We can work things out."

"Just get me the information, okay, Herb?"

"What exactly are you looking for? Lovers? Bad debts? Messy divorces?"

"I'm not sure what I'm looking for, but any of those three might explain a few things. See what you can find out."

Dixon grumbled. "All right. I owe you. I'll give you a call as soon as I've got anything useful. But in the meantime, Chance, will you do me a favor and rethink your decision to leave Dixon Security?"

"We've already been through this, Herb. I've told you my terms. Let me have another crack at the Truett & Tully case, and I'll give you six more months before I resign. Otherwise my resignation is effective as of the last time we spoke. Take it or leave it."

"You've never heard the word compromise, have you?"

"Nope. By the way, don't call me, I'll call you." He shot a glance at his watch. "Sometime around five this afternoon. That should give you enough time."

"Five o'clock! How the hell am I supposed to find out anything in a few hours?"

"I know you, Herb. You've been sitting behind that desk a long time, but your brain hasn't been totally eaten away by balance statements and business politics. You can still track down information when you need it. I'll call you in a few hours."

Chance hung up the phone without waiting for a response. His patience was finally exhausted. Lord knew he had been indulgent and patient long enough. It was time to stop fooling around with the subject of Rachel Wilder. Once he had some hard answers he would know exactly how to handle her.

When he knew the lady's secrets, he would have her where he wanted her.

7

RACHEL MADE THE DRIVE into town in something of a haze. She paid the necessary attention to her driving, but her mind was elsewhere. She parked the car in the lot of the town's one small supermarket and automatically started for the entrance without any clear idea of exactly what she intended to buy.

Going into town for groceries had been a temporary and short-lived escape. That was all. She didn't dare try to disappear this soon. All of Chance's hunting instincts would be aroused, and he would do as he threatened; he would follow her. Rachel had enough respect for his professional abilities to believe he would find her. He had convinced her of that.

She was so preoccupied wondering exactly how and when to plan her permanent escape from Snowball's Chance that she didn't see Keith Braxton until she collided with him at the entrance to the supermarket. One glance told her that his pleasant-faced veneer had been stripped away. She was seeing the side of him she'd only had a hint of the day she'd had lunch with him.

"Just the little housekeeper I've been wanting to see," Keith said with cool anticipation as he reached out to steady her. "I've been waiting for you."

Rachel looked up at him in startled confusion. "Waiting for me?"

"Yeah. You've been coming into town almost every day. I figured you'd probably come in today. I kept an eye on the turnoff to Snowball's Chance this morning and, sure enough, here you are. I followed you all the way into town, and you didn't even notice me in your rearview mirror. What's the matter, Rachel? Got too many other things on your mind these days?"

"Such as?" she snapped, thoroughly annoyed with him for turning into a pest. As if she didn't have enough problems at the moment.

"Such as your sister, Gail Vaughan," Keith said smoothly.

The shock went straight to the core. Rachel could hardly breathe. "How do you know about Gail?"

"The day we had lunch I went through your purse while you used the ladies' room," Keith said carelessly.

"My purse! How dare you?" Then she remembered the glass of water he'd spilled that day and realized it hadn't been an accident. "You're a bastard, Keith, but I suppose you already know that."

He paid no attention to her furious protest. "I found a few names and addresses that, being the earnest, hardworking journalist that I am, I ran down without too much difficulty. When I hit Gail Vaughan, I hit pay dirt. The old phone number you had for her was at Truett & Tully. When I called I was told she didn't work there any longer. A little more digging turned up the fact that she'd been asked to resign because of the results of an investigation carried out by an agent of Dixon Security. It didn't take any great intuitive leap to figure out that Abraham Chance was that agent." Keith smiled thinly. "Which left me with some very interesting questions about your presence at Snowball's Chance."

Rachel clutched the strap of her shoulder bag and gave him a scathing look. "Go ask your questions somewhere else. I'm not interested in talking to you." She started to walk around him, but he reached out and caught her arm.

"Not so fast, honey. You and I have some more talking to do, whether you like it or not."

"Forget it."

"Not possible. I've been after a good story on Chance for too long. All of a sudden I think I've found a brilliant angle, much better than the nice vanilla piece I was going to do about him being the perfect example of the modern, corporate samurai. I'm not about to walk away from it just because you don't feel like talking."

"What am I supposed to talk about?" she demanded angrily. "It sounds like you've already got all kinds of answers."

"Chance doesn't know who you are, does he?"

The first trickle of real fear went through her. Rachel did her best not to reveal it. "Of course he knows who I am."

Braxton shook his head. "Oh, he probably knows your name, but he doesn't know you're Gail Vaughan's sister, does he? He sure as hell wouldn't have hired you

as his housekeeper if he knew about that connection.
He's not stupid. And you're no housekeeper. Does he
know that?"

"Just what do you think I am, Braxton?" she asked
crisply.

His expression was one of infinite satisfaction.
"You're a sharp, successful planning analyst at a fast-
moving, fast-rising little industrial firm located in San
Francisco. You report to one of the firm's top executives, and you have your own secretary. Whatever else
you are, you, honey, are no housekeeper. And I'm
willing to bet my last dollar that Abraham Chance has
no idea who you really are and what you're really doing at Snowball's Chance. Because if he did he would
have torn you into little pieces by now. Chance does not
take kindly to being hoodwinked."

Braxton knew everything. Rachel fought to hold on
to her temper and her common sense. This whole thing
had been so terribly stupid. She rued the day Chance
had looked at her and called her a housekeeper. Even
more she rued her own foolish desire for revenge that
had convinced her to assume the role. She felt as if she
were watching the jaws of a very dangerous trap slowly
close around her. Everything that could go wrong had
gone wrong. All she could do now was try to fight a
rearguard action.

"Congratulations on your journalistic skills, Braxton," she said in a voice brittle with ice. "I don't see
what good the results are going to do you, but you're

welcome to them. Now if you'll excuse me, I've got some shopping to do."

His fingers tightened painfully on her arm. "We're not quite finished, you and I."

"I think we are." She tried to pull herself free and was enraged to discover he was gripping her so tightly she couldn't budge. "Let go of me before I call whatever passes for the local law around here."

He responded by yanking her toward him. "I said we're not quite finished, and I meant it. I can guess what you're doing at Snowball's Chance, Rachel. It's easy to figure out you're looking for something you can use against Chance. That's why you're masquerading as a housekeeper, isn't it? Housekeepers have access to all kinds of personal information about their employers. It was a stroke of luck that Chance needed someone to help him fix up that old house. It gave you the perfect opportunity to get close to him."

"You don't know what you're talking about."

"I'm not as blind as Chance apparently is," Braxton assured her. "And I think you and I can work together on this project. I'm after the same things you are, Rachel. I want inside information, something I can use to really punch up the article I'm going to do on him. If I handle it right, this piece could be really hot. I've got a much more interesting angle now, thanks to you."

Rachel glared at him. "Just what angle is that, Braxton?"

He grinned without any real humor. "Something along the lines of how one of Chance's victims feels when she takes a fall because of one of his investigations. Maybe I'll throw in some implication that seduction and betrayal were involved. Sex always sells. I'll paint Chance as a ruthless Romeo who seduces women to solve his cases. I like the sisterly revenge bit, too. That will add human interest. Readers will really eat up the intrigue, especially when I imply that you decided to pay Chance back in his own coin by seducing and then betraying him. Hell, this is big time. This might be more than a magazine piece. It might be a book."

Rachel could barely think. Desperately she tried to pull herself together. "You're stupid as well as being a bastard, aren't you, Braxton?"

"I might be a bastard, but I definitely am not stupid. Why fight me, honey? We're both on the same side. We both want an angle to use against Chance and, thanks to you, we've got it."

"My business with Abraham Chance has nothing to do with you."

"Ah, but it does." Braxton leaned forward to drive home his next words. "If you don't give me what I want by way of information and inside details, I'm going straight to Chance himself with the big news about just who his housekeeper really is."

"There's a name for that kind of threat," Rachel said.

"I know. It's called blackmail."

"You're out of your mind."

"Am I?" Braxton shook his head. "I don't think so. I think you'll agree to help me this time around. You don't want to take the risk of Chance learning who you are until you've evened the score with him for what he did to your sister."

"What makes you think he did anything to my sister?"

Braxton shrugged. "It's the only scenario that fits your presence here as Chance's so-called housekeeper. There's no other reason for you to try a deception like that unless you're out to do a little in-depth digging on the subject of Abraham Chance. The only thing that would have made you take this kind of risk is a desire for sweet revenge."

"What happens if I decide to let you go ahead and tell him the truth about who I am?" she challenged furiously.

Braxton smiled again. "That's easy. If you don't help me I'll do the story my way. And in the process I'll smear your sister's name from one end of the article to the other. I'll take some heavy swipes at yours, too. By the time I've finished, you and your sister will look like a couple of conniving, two-bit tramps. But if you help me, Rachel, I'll make your sister look like the injured party. I'll paint her as the innocent victim of a ruthless investigation by a man who was intent only on finding someone on whom Dixon Security could pin the blame. If you help me, I'll give you the revenge you want against Abraham Chance. If you refuse to help me, you and your sister will both take the same ride I'm going to give Chance. How's that for a bargain?"

Rachel looked down at where his fingers were closed roughly around her arm. "If you've finished outlining your threats, would you please release me, Braxton? I told you, I have shopping to do."

Braxton hesitated, trying to read the expression in her eyes. Then he smiled slowly and let her go. "You're a cool little customer, aren't you? But, then, I guess you'd have to be to pull off the housekeeper stunt."

Rachel said nothing. She turned on her heel and started blindly for the entrance of the supermarket.

"You'll help me, won't you, Rachel?" Braxton said softly behind her.

She kept walking.

"I know you will. As soon as you've had an opportunity to calm down and think about it, you'll see that helping me is the way to go. You'll get what you want out of this, and I'll get what I want."

Rachel pushed open the glass door and let it swing shut behind her. She never once looked back. Automatically she grabbed a cart and started down the nearest aisle. She had never been more grateful for the routine of grocery shopping in her life. Without thinking about what she was doing, she began picking up vegetables, stuffing them into little plastic bags and dropping them into the cart. Her conscious thoughts were all on the enormity of the mess she had created for herself and her stepsister.

Things had been bad before for Gail, but they would be a great deal worse if Keith Braxton wrote his article with a slant that would further blacken Gail's name.

Rachel knew he had probably meant it when he assured her he would drag her name through the mud in the process.

The alternative was to let Braxton have all the information he wanted on Chance and let Chance take the fall.

But she had already abandoned the notion of revenge. Chance might have made a serious mistake about Gail's involvement in the theft at Truett & Tully, and there was no doubt that he was a hard man, but Rachel no longer believed he had deliberately framed her sister. He was definitely not a kind or sympathetic man but he was an honest one and a proud one. There was a solid core of integrity in him. Rachel knew she had no right to seek vengeance against Chance.

All of which left her with only one option, she realized somewhere around the dairy department. She would have to do the one thing she had almost done that morning before Melinda arrived. She would have to tell Chance the whole story and let the chips fall where they might.

He was probably going to turn savage.

At the checkout stand, Rachel was stunned by the bill. She saw the number of bags of groceries she had unwittingly purchased while her mind had been churning with more important thoughts, and she groaned. She had just bought enough food to feed a small army.

At least no one was going to have to do any grocery shopping for a while. Maybe Chance would want to freeze some of the food after he'd kicked his erstwhile housekeeper out of the house.

Rachel drove back to Snowball's Chance determined to speak to Chance immediately and get the whole, outrageous confession behind her once and for all. She was so psyched up for the confrontation that she was taken totally by surprise when she pulled into the drive and saw another car beside Melinda's vehicle. Her employer was standing in the middle of the drive, his legs braced and his arms crossed in a pose of stubborn resistance.

He was surrounded by three people who all appeared to be talking at once. Chance's face was set. He looked at once beleaguered and militant. When he saw Rachel's Toyota, he also looked vastly relieved.

"About time you got back," he announced, dropping his arms to stride briskly through the small knot of people. They scattered out of his path like so much confetti. He reached down and opened Rachel's car door. "I'm paying for the services of a housekeeper, and I'd like to get my money's worth. Do something about all these people, will you? I've got work of my own to do."

Rachel's eyes went slowly from his grimly set face to the uncertain faces of the three people behind him. One of the group was Melinda. The handsome, dark-haired man next to her and the older woman with the neat, stylish haircut and anxious eyes were strangers. Rachel was overcome by a strong sense of foreboding. "Who are they?"

"In addition to my flighty sister, you are looking at the next great American novelist, Roarke Torrance, currently unemployed and unpublished. The other newcomer is my mother, Beth Chance. Mindy somehow succeeded in convincing both of them to come up here and help her plead her case. I'm ready to toss the lot of them down the mountain. Do something with them."

Rachel swallowed, seeing the hopeful, curious expressions on the faces of the other three. Her eyes flashed to Chance's face. "Chance, I want to talk to you."

"Later. Get these three off my back first."

"How?"

"How should I know? Give them a cup of coffee or something. You're the housekeeper around here."

Rachel's mouth went dry. "Chance, that's sort of what I wanted to talk to you about. Couldn't we . . ."

His eyes narrowed as he looked down at her. "I said later. Feed these three and calm them down. I've got too much to do. I can't afford to be pestered by a bunch of uninvited guests." He tugged her firmly out of the car. "You can start by getting them to help take in the groceries." He scanned the row of packages on the back seat. "Good Lord, it looks like you were planning to feed half the county."

"I got a little carried away," Rachel began awkwardly. "You see, I had some things on my mind when I went into the store, and I . . ." She broke off as Chance signaled the good-looking young man standing with his sister.

"You might as well make yourself useful, Torrance. Come on over here and give my housekeeper a hand with the groceries. Her name is Rachel, by the way. Rachel," he added, nodding toward the older woman, "this is Beth." He stepped away from the car, clearly washing his hands of the whole situation. "Excuse me, everyone, I've got work to do." He turned and stalked off toward the coach house without a backward glance.

"Chance, wait, we came here to talk to you," Melinda wailed helplessly.

"Later," he called over his shoulder.

Melinda shot a resentful glance at her mother. "Later means never."

Beth Chance smiled sympathetically at her daughter. "I told you this wasn't going to work, dear. You know Chance is not easily pressured."

"I'm not trying to pressure him, I'm trying to make him see sense," Melinda declared petulantly. "I have a right to control my own money."

"Well," Roarke Torrance said gamely as he smiled at Rachel, "we might as well get these groceries into the house. Almost lunchtime."

Rachel blinked at the barely concealed hint. Roarke Torrance had the look of a still-growing boy, even though he must be twenty-three or twenty-four at least. "Thank you," she said dryly as he reached down for the first sack of groceries. Belatedly she turned to Beth Chance.

"How do you do, Mrs. Chance? Sorry about all the confusion. I had no idea you were due to arrive. Chance didn't tell me he was expecting anyone."

Beth's eyebrows climbed upward as she slanted a quick, regretful glance at her daughter. "I'm afraid that was our fault, not Chance's. Melinda thought things might work better if we, uh, surprised her brother. Her plan was to come up here first and sort of, uh, soften him up. We were to follow and show him how much we support her. But I have a feeling it wasn't a good idea. Chance doesn't particularly care for surprises."

Melinda snatched up a sack of groceries. "He's an unfeeling, uncaring, cold-blooded bastard."

"Take it easy, Mindy," Roarke advised with a quiet firmness that surprised Rachel. "You've got to admit, you've taken him unawares by bringing me and your mother here like this. Can't blame him for being a little put out."

Rachel looked at Melinda. "Exactly what did you hope to accomplish?"

Melinda sighed. "I hoped that if the three of us confronted him all at once, we might be able to make him see reason."

Beth Chance shook her head. "Nothing else you've ever done has succeeded in getting him to turn over your money, dear. I don't know why I let you talk me into this fiasco. I doubt if it will work, either."

Melinda grimaced. "I'd think you'd be on my side, Mom. After all, he still controls your money, too."

"Only because I prefer it that way," Beth said soothingly. "I have no head for finances, and your father knew it. That's why he left Chance in charge of my trust fund."

"Well, I do have a head for money, and I want what's mine. Roarke and I are going to need it." Melinda stomped off toward the house with a sack of groceries in her arms.

Roarke watched her go and smiled fleetingly. "She's a little temperamental."

"I've noticed," Rachel said blandly. She started toward the house carrying two sacks. "Will you all be staying for dinner?"

Beth laughed. "Melinda is planning for all of us to spend the night."

"The night! Good grief, I'll have to get the other bedrooms ready. They're a mess. Haven't been used in years." Rachel was taken aback by the news. She would need all afternoon to get the extra bedrooms into any kind of shape. "And there's only one working bathroom...."

"Don't worry about it," Beth advised gently. "If I know Chance he's going to pack all three of us off to the nearest motel. He's up here to work, not entertain houseguests."

"But you're family."

"Somehow I don't think that's going to make a hell of a lot of difference," Roarke murmured. "I've only known Chance for about ten and a half minutes, but already I get the strong impression he doesn't take kindly to having his privacy invaded on such short notice. Melinda really goofed this time around. I should have known her scheme wasn't going to work."

Beth chuckled ruefully. "I've known from the beginning it probably wasn't going to work, but here I am. It's hard to resist getting caught up in my daughter's little scenes."

"Tell me about it." Roarke grinned. "One of these days I'm going to have to take a firm hand with that woman."

"Lots of luck," Beth said with deep meaning. "Chance is the only one I've known until now whom she couldn't wrap around her little finger. I'm afraid her inability to get her way with him makes her resort to desperate measures."

Roarke looked thoughtful. "You've got to admit, the money is hers. And in a few more months she's going to be twenty-one. She's got a good case for wanting to control her own trust fund. It's old-fashioned and chauvinistic to think women can't handle money as well as men."

"My husband was afraid that, left to her own devices, Mindy would run through the entire capital in no time," Beth said.

"Who knows what she'd do?" Roarke asked pleasantly as he walked up the front steps. "Mindy isn't stupid. If she suddenly had control of her own money, she might develop a stronger sense of responsibility toward it."

Rachel wondered about that. She also wondered how objective Roarke Torrance was likely to be on the subject of who controlled Melinda's trust. If Melinda was pregnant, and if she and Roarke were going to get married for the baby's sake, and if Roarke didn't have a job, things could get very tight financially.

Rachel switched the subject as she led the way into the house. She had her own problems to deal with, and she couldn't afford to become involved in a whole new set of problems.

Chief among her problems was finding a way to talk to Chance in private.

That proved futile. As the afternoon wore on, she realized it was going to be impossible to corner Chance until Melinda, Beth and Roarke were gone.

Being unable to confront him was having a devastating effect on her mental state, Rachel discovered as she started preparations for dinner. She was the type who preferred to get bad news and unpleasant scenes over with as quickly as possible.

She didn't have Gail's or Mindy's sense of the dramatic, apparently. Either of those two young women could wallow indefinitely in melodrama and tears. The thought made Rachel realize just how many similarities there were between Gail and Mindy.

And that made her realize how much she herself had in common with Chance. Both of them had been handed the responsibility of taking care of spoiled younger sisters years ago, and both of them were still struggling to carry out that responsibility in the best way they could.

Rachel sighed. She doubted that Chance would see the similarities in their situations. He wouldn't suddenly find himself filled with the gentle warmth of human understanding. He was more likely to wring her neck when he found out exactly where Rachel's sense of responsibility had led her. She looked down at her fingers holding a paring knife and saw that her hand was shaking. The problem was that when she'd returned from town, she'd been psyched up for the big scene.

Around five o'clock, when Chance entered the kitchen through the back door, she jumped in surprise. The knife she'd been using to pare vegetables clattered into the sink. He eyed her consideringly.

"What's the matter with you, Rachel? This crowd making you nervous?"

He was the one making her nervous, she thought resentfully. Then she realized it was the first time she'd been alone with him since her return from town. "It's not your guests," she began quickly.

"I don't know why not. They sure make me nervous." Chance stripped off his dirt-stained shirt. "I feel like Snowball's Chance has been besieged by the enemy." He glanced at the sink full of vegetables. "I take it they're all staying for dinner?"

"That was my understanding," Rachel said formally. "I got a couple more rooms ready upstairs. Fortunately I washed all those old sheets the other day. They're fairly tattered, but at least they're clean."

"Nobody's going to have to worry about the condition of the sheets. This lot is staying at a motel tonight."

Rachel looked at him skeptically. "Is that right?"

"Yes, it's right," he shot back. "I intend for us to have some privacy tonight, Rachel. You and I are going to talk, remember?"

She took a deep breath. "I know you said something about that, and as it happens, I—"

"Besides," he cut in, impatient with her small interruption, "Snowball's Chance is not yet in any condition to have houseguests. For Pete's sake, we've only got one working bathroom. Even if the place was ready, I definitely am not. I've got more important things to handle."

Rachel froze at the expression in his eyes. Maybe it would be best to simply make a run for it, after all. She didn't want to deal with what was going to come down on her head after she'd told Chance the whole truth and then warned him about Keith Braxton.

"When's dinner?" Chance asked in the short, taut silence that followed his comment.

"At six."

He nodded. "Fine. I'll tell Beth she'd better get busy and make reservations at a motel in town. I'd just as soon get the three of them off this hill before it gets too late. There's another storm on the way, and this one's going to be packing some real wind and rain." He started for the door. "I've got to make a phone call, and then I'm going to take a shower. Have my drink waiting when I'm finished, will you? I've had a hard day."

The casually arrogant demand succeeded in pushing Rachel over the edge of the precarious emotional precipice on which she'd been balanced for hours. She picked up the knife and sliced ruthlessly into a potato. "You're not the only one who's had a hard day, Chance. It's been a little rough all around. I could use a good stiff drink myself. Furthermore, I'd like to point out that you have a very undiplomatic way of giving orders, do you know that? No wonder Mrs. Vinson split as soon as she could. It's a miracle anyone is willing to work for you."

"You work for me, don't you, Rachel?" he tossed back laconically. "Since you dislike the job so much, it makes me wonder why you took it in the first place."

She flinched and then glared at him. He was baiting her, and the knowledge was infuriating. She hated this cat-and-mouse game he seemed to have invented. "I must be a glutton for punishment."

"I don't think so," he retorted softly. "I think you're just a little too reckless for your own good, and I think you may be in more trouble than you can handle, but I don't think you're a glutton for punishment. You're much too gutsy to play the masochist long."

"I appreciate the psychological analysis," she said tightly, turning back to the sink.

"You might as well pour yourself a drink when you pour mine," Chance said behind her. "You're right.

You're going to need it." He walked out of the kitchen before Rachel could say another word.

Rachel stood still for a long moment, gazing unseeingly down at the vegetables. What the heck, she told herself with sudden decision. It was a long-standing tradition for housekeepers to take a little nip from the employer's liquor supply. Who was she to fly in the face of tradition? She put down the knife, walked over to the cupboard where Chance kept the bottle of Scotch and opened the door.

The smooth fire of twelve-year-old Scotch went a long way toward settling her nerves.

DINNER PASSED in a mixture of false cheeriness and awkward conversation between Beth, Roarke and Rachel. Melinda confined her comments to needling remarks on the subject of tight-fisted, arrogant brothers.

Chance sat at the head of the table with a stoic expression on his face and managed to stay above it all. He responded occasionally to Beth's efforts at polite conversation, and he even unbent so far as to discuss plumbing repairs with Roarke when the younger man revealed an unexpected knowledge of the subject. But he ignored Melinda altogether until after dinner. At that point he looked point-blank at her and announced it was time for her to leave.

"But, Chance, Rachel's fixed up the bedrooms upstairs. There's no reason we can't stay here," Melinda announced, digging in for the final battle. "We're family."

"You're staying at the motel, and that's final. I've had enough houseguests for one day, and I didn't hire Rachel to cook and clean for three other people."

"Well, what did you hire her for?" Melinda said with sudden spitefulness. "Does she have a lot of other *domestic* talents?"

There was a shocked, embarrassed pause as everyone went silent. Chance's eyes glittered as he turned on his sister. "You will apologize for that remark, or I'll see to it you never get your hands on that trust fund money if you live to be a hundred."

Melinda stared at him in horror, apparently realizing that he meant it. "You can't do that, Chance," she whispered, but her voice was weak.

"Try me."

Melinda burst into tears. It seemed to be her usual recourse when things became too much for her to handle. Gail had the same talent, Rachel reflected.

"I didn't mean it," Melinda said through her sniffles. "I'm sorry, Rachel, really I am. I'm just so mad at Chance, I can't seem to help myself. It was a thoughtless thing to say."

"It's all right," Rachel said woodenly, turning away with a stack of dishes in her hands. She knew her cheeks were fiery red. "Forget it."

It was Roarke who got to his feet with abrupt determination. "That does it, Mindy. You've finally gone a little too far. Get your things. We're leaving." He paid no attention to Melinda's desperate attempt to change his mind. "Beth, you drive your car. I'll take Mindy in mine. I have a few things to say to her. We'd better get going. That wind is starting to howl out there. The rain will be here any minute." He started toward the kitchen door, dragging Melinda along by her wrist.

Chance watched first in astonishment and then with something that might have been approval. Beth smiled at her son.

"I meant to tell you, Chance. I rather like Roarke."

"I think I'm beginning to see why," Chance said slowly. He pushed back his chair and got to his feet. "Take it easy on the drive back to town, Beth. When the weather turns nasty, the road turns to mud. Roarke's right. If you leave now you should be able to get out ahead of the rain."

"We're on our way, although knowing Melinda, we'll probably be back first thing in the morning. She's very determined, Chance." Beth shook her head. "She wants to marry Roarke, and he's told her they have to wait until he gets through grad school and lines up a job."

"And as usual, Mindy doesn't want to wait for anything," Chance observed.

"She thinks that if she can convince you to turn her money over to her, she'll be able to convince Roarke not to wait any longer. He can devote himself to his graduate work or, better yet his writing, and she'll be able to play at being his wife."

"She's spoiled rotten, you know," Chance said coolly. Without any warning he swung his biting gaze on Rachel. "Rachel has a younger sister, too, don't you, Rachel?"

Rachel's startled eyes flashed up to meet his. "Yes."

"Is she as spoiled and willful and dramatic as Melinda?"

Rachel struggled for breath. Her throat felt tight. Desperately she wondered why he was suddenly targeting her stepsister. "My sister has been through a lot lately," she managed with as much dignity as possible. *And so have I,* she added silently. She longed for another shot of Scotch.

"What did you say her name was, Rachel?" Chance prompted softly.

Frantically Rachel tried to remember the name she'd given Chance the first time the subject of her stepsister had arisen.

"Anna," she said so quietly that she didn't think either Chance or his mother had heard.

"Yes, Anna," Chance repeated slowly.

"Well, we'd best be on our way." Beth gave Chance an affectionate peck on the cheek and turned to smile at Rachel. "It was a lovely dinner, Rachel. Sorry to leave you with all the dishes."

"It's what she gets paid for," Chance said grimly. "You know me, Beth. I always like to get my money's worth. Good night. Try to keep Melinda headed back toward San Francisco, okay?"

"I'll try, but it won't be easy."

Rachel worked furiously in the kitchen, thankful for the pile of dishes waiting to be washed as she listened to the leave-taking in the hall. After what seemed an endless pause, the engines of two cars finally came alive out in the drive. The front door closed, and then there was silence. An ominous, dangerous sort of silence.

Rachel felt very alone in the kitchen. When she sensed Chance's presence in the doorway behind her, she found herself gripping the edge of the sink for support.

"Now," Chance said calmly, "we talk."

Rachel never knew what she would have said next, because almost immediately both cars returned to the driveway outside.

"What the hell...?" Chance swung around and headed for the door. "If Mindy thinks she can talk her way into staying here, after all, she's got another think coming."

But it was Roarke standing at the door a moment later. He gave Chance a wry, apologetic look. "Sorry about this. There's a tree down across the road. Going to be a chore to move it in this wind and rain. I don't think we can get out of here until morning."

Rachel went to stand in the kitchen doorway, a strange, cowardly sense of relief washing over her. She didn't have to be alone with Chance tonight, after all. "Good thing I got those bedrooms ready this afternoon, isn't it?" she said with the unnatural cheerfulness of a woman who has just been granted a reprieve.

8

IT TOOK THE HOUSE hours to settle down into darkness and sleep. The sheer logistical problems presented by one bathroom and five adults helped drag out the seemingly endless process. It was nearly midnight before everyone was in bed.

Rachel lay cuddled beneath her quilt, listening to the new silence and the rain outside her window, and told herself reprieves were double-edged swords. They merely postponed the inevitable, and postponement could be a form of torture in and of itself. Sooner or later she had to talk to Chance, and she knew it. She faced that fact with typical, unflinching determination.

Nevertheless, a part of her was definitely grateful to have a few more hours to marshal her explanations and her arguments. She had seen how cold and hard Chance could be when he chose. There was no reason he should go easy on Rachel when she finally told him what was happening. She was far too realistic to believe that his making love to her last night would influence him tomorrow.

She sighed and turned on her side, wondering if the rain was slowing somewhat. It seemed to her that it had rained nearly every night she'd been at Snowball's

Chance. Normally she didn't mind rain, but tonight it added an element of gloominess to the atmosphere that made her even more restless. She knew now why the service station attendant, before giving her directions to Snowball's Chance, had found it easy to pretend the place was haunted when he was a kid. It didn't take a lot of imagination to envision a specter or two hovering on the sagging balcony outside her bedroom.

Rachel's nerves were strung so tightly that when she saw the door of her room open and close in near silence, she almost screamed.

"Don't," Chance advised dryly. "You'll wake them all up again, and I'm not sure I could handle the uproar." He came toward the bed, moving with his nearly silent stride. He was still wearing his jeans, but that was all he had on. In the shadowed gloom he seemed too big and very dangerous.

Rachel sat bolt upright in bed, clutching the sheet and quilt to her chin. "What are you doing here?"

"Don't embarrass both of us with silly questions." He sank down on the edge of the bed, putting a severe depression in the old mattress. "I've had enough silliness today." He didn't touch her, but his eyes gleamed in the darkness. "You know what I'm doing here. Did you think I was going to put off our little talk for another day?"

Rachel edged backward until she was partly braced against the wall on her side of the bed. "Let's just say I had hopes," she murmured.

His sleekly muscled shoulders shifted in a minimal shrug. His eyes never left her face. "You should have known me better than that."

"Yes. I should have." She ducked her head for a moment, instinctively seeking shelter behind the wings of her hair while she gathered her thoughts.

"Don't hide from me, Rachel." The words were half command, half coaxing reassurance. Chance put out his hand and tipped up her chin so that she was again forced to meet his eyes. "You're not the kind of woman who hides from anything."

"I don't think you know how intimidating you can be."

His hand fell away. "Tell me everything, Rachel. I want to know why you're here, why you're pretending to be a housekeeper and what it is that upset you so much in town today."

She stared at him. "You knew?"

"That something happened when you went into town? Oh, yes. I knew. I'm beginning to know you very well, Rachel Wilder. You're going to find it harder and harder to keep your secrets from me."

She might as well get this over and done. Rachel took a deep breath and then said bluntly, "I'm Gail Vaughan's stepsister."

"Gail Vaughan." Chance spoke the name in an utterly neutral tone of voice. He said nothing else, but his eyes were brilliant and piercing as he focused on Rachel's face.

"Don't you even remember her?" Rachel asked a little sharply.

"I remember her."

"You should. You accused her of selling Truett & Tully's corporate secrets to its competitors. You were the investigator Dixon Security sent in to solve the case, and Gail was the one you nailed for the crime. She lost her job, which she happened to love. She lost a lot more in the process. She became very depressed, lost her self-confidence, her faith in human nature and generally came apart."

"She was lucky she was given the chance to resign instead of being fired outright or taken to court."

Rachel winced at the chilled tone. "There wasn't much choice, was there?"

"As I said, she was fortunate."

"You really are as hard as iron, aren't you?"

"Go on with your story, Rachel."

Her fingers clenched the soft fabric of the quilt. "My sister was innocent."

"Was she?"

"Yes, she was," Rachel said through gritted teeth. "She's very young in some ways, a little immature, rather like . . . like your sister, I imagine. But she is not a thief!"

"There was a great deal of evidence against her," Chance pointed out emotionlessly.

"I know. She told me. She also told me she'd been set up."

Chance drummed his fingers in a short, intense pattern on his thigh. He stopped the unconscious movement almost immediately. "Tell me about it."

This was going to be the hard part. Rachel summoned up all her courage. "She told me that you'd been the one to plant the evidence."

There was an awful stillness in him. "Did she?"

Rachel waited for the denial. When it wasn't forthcoming she plunged on. "She told me that you had . . . had seduced her. Put her off guard and then framed her. When the evidence was found, you advised her to resign. She was stunned. She didn't know what else to do, so she obeyed when Ed Fraley, her boss, confronted her. She handed in her resignation. The next thing she knew she was out on the street, you were nowhere to be found, and Dixon Security was declaring the case successfully closed."

"An interesting summary of events. Tell me why you came to Snowball's Chance, Rachel."

"Isn't that obvious?" she asked with as much coolness as she could manage. "I came here with some idea of telling you exactly what I thought of you. I had some vague notion of threatening you with a lawsuit or something. I wanted to punish you. I wanted revenge for what you'd done to my sister."

"Ah." There was a wealth of comprehension in the single, drawn-out sound.

"I didn't know how I was going to get it. I had vague ideas of going to the press, but I doubted they would believe me or even be interested enough to pursue it. I thought about suing you. I thought about trying to cloud your name the way my sister's has been clouded. But most of all I wanted to confront you and tell you what a bastard I thought you were. I had some vacation time coming, so I took it and came after you."

"You took some time off from work, packed an overnight bag and came looking for the monster who had seduced your sister and set her up to take the fall at Truett & Tully," Chance concluded thoughtfully. "You arrived, and I mistook you for the housekeeper I'd given up on getting."

"The opportunity seemed too good to pass up," Rachel admitted. "I didn't know how I was going to use the position, but the thought of being able to get to know you and perhaps learn something I could use against you was too tempting. I went along with your assumption."

"The fact is, you aren't too bad as a housekeeper," Chance noted with critical satisfaction. "I detected a few signs of obvious corporate management techniques where I least expected them, a touch of temperament, a tendency toward bossiness and a certain independence, but on the whole you got the job done."

"Not quite."

He nodded. "You're right. You didn't quite get the job done. You didn't take your revenge, did you? Why not, Rachel? Couldn't you figure out a way to get at me?"

She wished he wouldn't talk in that icy-cold, emotionless tone. It disturbed her deeply. She couldn't tell what he was thinking. She could only surmise that he was furious. "I found a way," she said softly. "But I discovered I couldn't use it."

His look sharpened. "Why not?"

Rachel sighed. "Because even though you were wrong about my sister, I don't think you set her up the way she said you did."

"You don't believe I seduced her and then planted the evidence against her?"

Rachel shook her head. "No. You're a hard man, Chance. And you're not a particularly kind person. You're impatient with people who don't function the way you think they should, such as your own sister. You're a lot of the things Mrs. Vinson claimed. Rude, arrogant, dictatorial. But ..."

"But what?"

"But you're fundamentally honest. You have a streak of integrity that's a yard deep and a mile wide. Too wide to allow you to seduce and frame an innocent woman just so you could claim you'd solved a case. It would be beneath you to do something like that. I'm convinced now that you turned Gail over to the wolves because you truly believed she was the guilty party in that sordid mess."

"An interesting conclusion," he murmured. "So you decided I might be a little slow and stupid as an investigator, but I wasn't deliberately corrupt."

Rachel flushed. "I realize the evidence against my sister was very strong."

"It was," he confirmed dryly. "I've got a hunch you don't know just how strong it was. But you decided to abandon your notions of revenge because you no longer believed that I had deliberately ruined Gail's career at Truett & Tully. Interesting. Go on, Rachel. I get the feeling this isn't the end of the story. Something happened last night after we made love, didn't it? Something you wanted to talk about. What was it?"

Rachel bent her knees, pulling them up to her breasts beneath the covers and wrapping her arms around them. "I guess I wanted to believe that you were a kinder man than I had originally thought. I had some notion of asking you to reopen the case against my sister. I wanted you to make some further inquiries and see if you couldn't find the real culprit."

There was a long silence from Chance before he said softly, "You're convinced she's innocent."

"Absolutely."

"And you were going to ask me for help. Then my sister arrived and gave you the distinct impression I wasn't in the charity business."

"I decided I should probably just cut my losses and leave. But something else happened, Chance. You're not going to like this part."

"That doesn't surprise me. I haven't liked much of this so far. Tell me the rest of it, Rachel."

"Soon after I got here that reporter called. The one you told me might pester you," she began cautiously.

"Hell." The quiet violence in the muttered oath gave the impression that Chance had already leaped ahead to the obvious conclusion. "He talked you into meeting him?"

"I agreed to talk to him and then changed my mind after I hung up the phone. Unfortunately, I didn't know how to reach him and explain that I wanted to cancel the meeting. So I went to it. I, uh, pleaded housekeeper's ethics or something and told him I really couldn't talk about you. At the time he seemed very nice. He gave up graciously and said he understood. But I was wrong about him. He hadn't given up at all. He researched me and found out who I was. The man had the gall to go through my purse while I was in the ladies' room!"

"A journalist's ethics are slightly different from a housekeeper's ethics," Chance said as if he found her momentary outrage almost amusing. "Theirs are quite a bit lower on the scale, in fact. Nonexistent in some cases."

"This morning when I went into town for groceries he . . . he tailed me and confronted me in the supermarket parking lot." Rachel closed her eyes briefly. "He told me he knew all about Gail and what had happened at Truett & Tully. He had figured out why I was at Snowball's Chance. He said that if I didn't help him do the story on you, he would write it in such a way that Gail's name would be dragged publicly through the mud. Mine, too, for good measure."

"And if you helped him with inside information, he would write the story in a way that would just hurt my reputation and not hers and yours, right?"

"I guess that about sums it up," she agreed quietly.

"Then you told him to shove it and came home to confess everything to me," he finished for her.

"You can't give in to blackmailers," Rachel said with dignity. "When I got back here, though, the place was full of people, and there wasn't any privacy. And you suddenly seemed determined to confront me about the fact that I wasn't a professional housekeeper. Everything seemed to be closing in on me, and now that I was living under a blackmail threat I couldn't just disappear. Braxton knew who I was and where I lived. He could have found me easily."

"He wasn't the only one threatening to come after you."

"No," she agreed, remembering Chance's promise to pursue her if she tried to escape.

"Any way you look at it, you were caught in a trap and the door was closing."

"It must have been how my sister felt when she was framed at Truett & Tully," Rachel said bleakly.

"We'll get into that later." Chance showed absolutely no sign of sympathy. "Right now let's stick to your problems."

"I've told you everything, Chance. It's a mess, and I'm sorry about parts of it, but parts of it aren't my fault."

He reached for her, pushing her down onto her back. Then he stretched out on top of the quilt and leaned over her. He slid his fingers deeply into her hair, anchoring her head on the pillow. "Not your fault, huh?"

She held on to her courage, not certain of what he intended. "It's true. I came looking for revenge, I'll admit."

"It was an honest desire for vengeance. I respect that. In your shoes, I would have done something similar," he said.

"I know," she whispered. "You aren't the kind of man to let a score go unsettled, are you?"

"No. You've learned a few things about me during the past few days, haven't you?"

She nodded, uncomfortably aware of the weight of him as he lay on top of the covers. The heavy quilt was pulled tightly around her, and he was holding it taut with the pressure of his body. So taut, in fact, that she could hardly move. She was cocooned in a soft but effective prison. "Yes, Chance, I've learned a few things about you."

"Enough to know I wouldn't have deliberately framed your sister."

"Enough to know that much," she agreed quietly. "I'm sorry about the mess I got into with Braxton, but it wasn't my fault he turned into a blackmailer. Besides, he was on your tail a long time before I came into the picture."

"You should never have met him for lunch," Chance stated flatly.

"Why not? He seemed nice enough at the time, and I had already decided not to spy on you for him."

"Maybe if I'd taken action then, he would have thought twice about trying blackmail," Chance said grimly.

Experimentally Rachel tried to move her legs beneath the confining quilt. She couldn't shift them more than a couple of inches. The feeling of being trapped was stronger than ever. "I don't understand," she whispered. "What action could you have taken? You didn't know anything about him or me at that point."

"I knew you were going into town for lunch, and I knew the name of the restaurant. I was going to go after you and see exactly what you were up to, but I made an unfortunate detour into the coach house."

Her eyes widened. "You were going to follow me? But how did you know about the restaurant?"

"You left the impression behind on the notepad where you jotted down the name of the place," he explained impatiently. "I'm supposed to be a trained investigator, remember?" His voice was full of self-derision. "And I knew you weren't a professional housekeeper in spite of your tendency to discard every useful thing you come across in a closet or cupboard. Admittedly, I've been a little slow getting around to unraveling your secrets, but that was because I thought I had plenty of time. Initially I just wanted you to confide in me."

Rachel moistened her dry lips. "About what?"

He shrugged, his hands twisting absently in her hair. "About whatever had sent you looking for shelter at Snowball's Chance. I assumed you were running from something and had gotten word of this job privately through Mrs. Vinson. The day you went into town for lunch, however, I figured I'd better find out who you were meeting. The crack on the head from that old radiator put paid to that plan. By the time I woke up you were home."

"I didn't realize you were so suspicious of me." Rachel tried to free her arm of the quilt but found it trapped at her side. Chance seemed totally unaware of her small push for freedom. He was too intent on studying her shadowed face.

"Today I decided enough was enough. I phoned Herb Dixon and reminded him he owed me a favor or two. I had him run a check on you, and he turned up the connection with Gail Vaughan almost immediately."

"You *what*?" A wave of anger swept through her, driving out anxiety and despair and even guilt. "You ran a check on me? You had me investigated?"

"Before we sat down to dinner tonight I knew who you were and I'd figured out your being here had something to do with Gail," he confirmed ruthlessly.

"Well, why didn't you say that when you barged in here a few minutes ago?" she yelped. "Why did you let me tell you the whole story as if you didn't know who I was?"

"Because I wanted to hear the whole story from you. There was a lot I didn't know. There was the bit about Braxton, for instance. And the fact that you'd come looking for revenge but had given up the project when you'd decided I might be stupid but I wasn't corrupt.

I'm still not sure that's much of a compliment, by the way, but at least it tells me something about you."

"Like what?" she challenged furiously.

"Like the fact that you might be a little dumb, too, but you're basically honest. You wouldn't savage an innocent man. The fact that you didn't talk to Braxton about me the first time you met him is interesting. You really do have a streak of integrity, don't you? Even when you're looking for vengeance."

"You've been playing games with me," she accused tightly. "Cat-and-mouse games. First you tried to coax me into confiding in you and then you tried to follow me and finally you had me investigated. And all the while you treated me like the housekeeper I claimed to be. You treated me like a servant."

"Treating you like a real housekeeper was just a bit of poetic justice on my part. You're the one who chose the role, remember."

"If I could get my hands free of this quilt, I'd wrap them around your neck!"

"If it's any consolation, I've had a few semiviolent thoughts about you myself. But I much prefer to take out my frustrations this way." He bent his head and kissed her heavily.

Rachel struggled at first, a part of her furious at the way he had made her tell him the truth, even though he already knew a great deal of it.

But he was making love to her. Did that mean he'd forgiven her, she wondered desperately. She didn't know what to think, but her emotions were in a turmoil, and her body was aching to seize the passionate opportunity for release that Chance seemed to be offering.

She wanted him. But if desire was all she felt, she could have resisted him. The real problem was that she'd fallen in love with her intended victim, and the fact that he now knew the truth about her didn't change her feelings. She was angry at him, chagrined at the way he'd toyed with her this evening, but she was still in love with him. And he was offering her a way of indulging some of the tempestuous emotions that were roiling within her.

In any event, it was useless to struggle against the confinement of the quilt. She was completely trapped in its soft embrace, and she realized that Chance not only knew it, he was deliberately taking advantage of it.

His mouth moved druggingly on hers, urging her lips apart until, with a soft moan of surrender and desire, she opened her mouth and allowed him into her softness.

"Ah, Rachel," he breathed in satisfaction, and then he was leaning more heavily into her as he deepened the kiss.

Rachel could feel the weight of him, sensed the way his body was hardening as he claimed her with his thrusting, searching kiss. Whatever else had happened between them, he still wanted her. That realization gave her hope. It also further aroused her passion.

The quilt seemed more confining than ever. Rachel stirred beneath Chance's warm, overwhelming kiss, but she was still unable to move. Her head twisted restlessly on the pillow, and she heard his deep, dark laughter.

"What is it, sweetheart? What do you want?"

"Let me go," she pleaded in a breathless whisper.

"I'm not sure I dare set you free. You might brain me."

"No, I only want—"

"Yes," he prompted when she broke off, "what do you want, sweet Rachel?"

"I want to make love with you."

"What happened to wanting to have your revenge against me?"

"Don't tease me, Chance. I told you I no longer want revenge." She tried to turn beneath the quilt, striving to find some give in the prison of its thick folds. Then a thought struck her. Her eyes collided with his as he looked down at her. "Maybe I should ask you what you want of me. Is this your idea of punishment?"

He groaned. "Right now I've got better things to do than punish you, honey. Besides, the truth is, you only did what I would have done in similar circumstances. How can I blame you for that? I want you very badly, Rachel. I didn't know it was possible to want a woman this much." He slowly began to pull back the quilt.

She lay still as he freed her from the covers. He put his hand on her upper leg beneath the hem of her nightgown. Slowly his fingers traveled upward, carrying the cotton gown along. His palm glided warmly over her hip, across the curve of her stomach and up to a point just beneath her breasts. Rachel trembled.

"You're so soft," he murmured. He lowered his head and dropped a warm, damp kiss onto the skin of her bare stomach. When Rachel gasped his name and clutched at his head, he groaned and started trailing the kisses upward toward her breasts. The cotton gown was lifted free and tossed heedlessly on the floor beside the bed.

"Oh, Chance, I want you so," Rachel murmured again and again, her hands seeking the planes of his shoulders and back, then the hard, male buttocks. His leg moved over hers, pushing between her thighs so that she was forced to open herself to his touch.

When he found her breasts with his lips, Rachel sucked in her breath and arched herself against him. Then he began talking to her, the words compelling, fascinating, mesmerizing. The gravel in his deep voice was as hot as the fires of a volcano, and the tantalizing shards of ice only served to stir her senses. Rachel listened, her pulse racing with excitement as Chance told her all the delicious things he was going to do to her. He outlined the details of his forthcoming possession with a sexy, sensual explicitness that set Rachel's blood on fire. She would never have believed words alone could be so thrilling or could fill her with such a blazing, aching need.

She clung to him, breathing his name over and over even as her body pleaded with him for the final intimacy. "Please, Chance, please. Now. I need you. I want you."

"I know, sweetheart. I can feel how much you want me. Last night I discovered that you are a very honest creature in bed. Do you have any idea what it's like to know you want me like this?" His fingers probed gently between her legs, gliding through the humid warmth that was the indisputable evidence of her desire.

Chance moved against her hip, and Rachel realized with a start that he was still wearing his jeans. Her fingers went to his waist, fumbling with the fastening.

"I love the feel of your hands on me," he muttered as she pushed the denim down over his hips and discovered he wasn't wearing any underwear. "Touch me, Rachel. Hold me."

His hot, heavy manhood filled her hands, and she stroked him softly, listening to the deep, shuddering need in his voice. The fierceness of his response was intoxicating. She cupped him and drew her fingertip across the velvet-covered steel.

"Enough!" Chance jerked himself back out of her grasp, half groaning and half laughing as he did so. "Any more of that, and I'll go up in flames before I get inside you. And inside you is where I would much prefer to be." He eased himself away from her for a moment. Rachel heard him scrabbling about on the floor and knew he was reaching into the pocket of his jeans for a little foil packet.

When he was finished he came back in a heavy rush, moving over her, lifting her legs and parting them so that she was completely open to him. He slowly, deliberately brought himself against her, pausing at the entrance to her body so that she had time to feel the pulsating strength of his need.

Then he reached down and parted her with his fingers. He guided himself to her and surged forward until he was totally sheathed within her softness.

"Rachel, oh, my sweet, soft, hot Rachel." He buried his face in the curve of her neck and wrapped one hand around her buttocks. "I think I'm going to get addicted to the small sounds you make when I have you like this. Not to mention the way your whole body clings to me. I think I'm the one who's trapped."

"I'm glad," she whispered passionately, her arms holding him tightly as he began to move against her. "I want you to feel as trapped as I do."

It was the truth, she realized as she responded instantly to the rhythm he was establishing. She felt strangely bound to him, and she desperately wanted him to feel the same way. She needed to know he was as caught up in the glimmering coils of passion as she was.

But she stopped pondering the matter as Chance's lovemaking quickly precluded all extraneous thought. When he was deep within her like this, she could concentrate only on the shimmering promise and the glorious sense of completeness that enveloped her.

Her body began to grow taut with sensual tension that brought her close to the breaking point. Chance felt that and thrust more deeply, imprisoning her within his grasp as his own body tightened in anticipation.

The excitement swelled, overtaking them both in a wonderfully merciless explosion. Forgetting all about the potential listeners sleeping in the rooms up and down the hall of the old house, Rachel parted her lips to cry out.

Instantly Chance covered her mouth with his own, drinking the sweet, feminine sounds of completion and swallowing his own hoarse shout in the process.

Slowly they drifted down through the layers of excitement until they found the soft haven in the wake of satisfaction.

Peace settled on the room. Outside the rain began to slacken. Rachel stirred, and Chance reluctantly eased himself from her.

"Relax," he murmured in sleepy, amused tones. "I don't think we woke anyone."

"I hope not," Rachel said, thinking of how embarrassing and downright awkward it would be if anyone came knocking on the door. "I'd hate to have them all thinking you really were sleeping with your housekeeper."

"Why?" he asked, smoothing the hair back from her cheek.

"Well, it would be embarrassing. Especially after your sister's comments tonight on my, er, household duties."

"Forget Mindy." Chance leaned forward and kissed the tip of Rachel's nose. "Forget all of them. This is just between you and me."

"Well, I should hope so!"

He laughed softly. "Tomorrow we're going to get rid of the lot, and then I'm going to clean up a few stray details."

"What kind of details?" she asked anxiously.

"First of all, the kind of details Keith Braxton dragged into this. After that you and I are going to discuss your sister."

Rachel went still. Perhaps all was not forgiven, after all. "What are we going to discuss about Gail?"

"You," Chance informed her with a yawn, "are going to do what you almost did after the last time we were in bed together. You're going to ask me for help."

Rachel swallowed. "And will you give it to me?"

"I'll try, but it's going to take some doing. You're going to have to ask me very nicely."

Rachel propped herself up on her elbow and gazed down at him. He regarded her from beneath half-closed lids. "What do you mean it's going to take some doing? Because of the evidence against Gail?"

"No. I should be able to punch holes in that. If I get a little cooperation, that is. Gail never told you the whole story, it seems."

Rachel was growing frustrated. "What whole story?"

"The reason she took the rap for what was going on at Truett & Tully was because, when the evidence was discovered, she quietly confessed. That confession tied my hands. It satisfied Truett & Tully, and it satisfied my boss, who promptly pulled me off the case."

Rachel was stunned. "Confessed! Why on earth would she do a thing like that?" Gail had said nothing about confessing. But, then, Gail had lied about being seduced and framed by Chance, too. Rachel's head whirled.

"I wondered a lot about that at the time myself. I really pushed her about her so-called confession. I was almost sure she was lying, and I was madder than hell at being stopped just when I thought I was getting somewhere. But she insisted, and Truett & Tully was more than happy to have the case solved. So was Herb Dixon, for that matter. So your sister took the fall. And I quit my job with Dixon Security because Herb jerked me off the case. Herb likes things nice and neat. As it turned out, so did Truett & Tully. With your idiotic sister loudly proclaiming her guilt and crying her eyes red, there wasn't a whole hell of a lot I could do. So I walked away from the mess. I have no patience with bureaucratic politics or with martyrs, for that matter. I strongly suspect your sister was playing martyr. She has a streak of the melodramatic in her."

"Just like Mindy?"

"Afraid so." Chance rolled onto his side and pushed her gently back down on the pillow. "I can't abide wimpy females who use tears and dramatics to get through life. Give me a feisty, fighting type of woman— every time." He kissed Rachel soundly.

"Chance, we've got to talk."

"In the morning," he promised, and deepened the kiss.

Rachel sighed and surrendered.

9

HE OUGHT TO BE GRATEFUL for small favors, Chance thought as he opened his eyes the next morning. After all, here he was waking up beside Rachel after a night spent proving to himself and to her that she wanted him with all the passion in her complex soul.

He felt her stir slightly and snuggle more deeply into the curve of his body. The gentle, unconsciously sensual movement sent a wave of satisfaction through him. He was making progress. Deliberately he tried looking at the positive side of the ledger. Mentally he ticked off the important points.

Point number one was that Rachel had abandoned her plans for revenge after getting to know him. She'd done so in spite of the fact that at that point she still hadn't known the whole truth about her stepsister. Gail had never bothered to mention that she herself had confessed to the crime. Instead she had played on her sister's sympathies by claiming she'd been seduced and set up. It was nice to know that Rachel had developed enough faith in his integrity to believe he wouldn't have stooped to framing Gail. It was a beginning. Of course, there must be a lot more they *both* didn't know about Gail.

Point number two was that Rachel had resisted the urge to spy on him for Keith Braxton. All things considered, her decision in that regard didn't particularly surprise Chance. She was the kind of woman who would want her vengeance firsthand. She would want to make certain her victim knew exactly how, when and why. Rachel would want to look in his eyes when she took her revenge. She wouldn't turn the business over to a third party. Chance could have told her that much about herself if she'd ever bothered to ask, because he had recognized almost from the beginning that she had a few things in common with him.

Revenge was like love. It was not a spectator sport. Instinctively both of them recognized that elemental fact.

Okay, so far so good. Chance shifted his position carefully, letting his hand glide across Rachel's lusciously curved thigh. When she moved slightly beneath his touch, sleepily cradling herself deeper into his warmth, he halted the caress. He wasn't ready to waken her yet. He was still counting off positive points on the invisible ledger in his head. Thoughtfully he went on to item number three. He was deliberately trying to keep it at the bottom of the list, because he knew that if he focused on it too long it would blind him to all the rest.

Point number three was that Rachel responded to him with a sweet, hot sensuality that went to his head faster than the twelve-year-old Scotch he kept in the kitchen cupboard. Just thinking about her and what had happened between them during the night was enough to make his body harden all over again.

Fine. So he could add a strong sexual attraction to the list of positive points. Terrific.

Great.

Wonderful.

It wasn't enough. No matter how he looked at it, the list was not complete.

The raw truth was that he wanted far more from Rachel than her passion or her instinctive faith in his integrity. He was in love with her, and he wanted her to love him in return.

He didn't delude himself. Right now she was not at all certain of what she felt for him. Her passion for him was still offset by her wariness. Her trust in him was countered by her certainty that he was basically a hard and ruthless man. He hadn't done much lately to prove her wrong.

All things considered, he thought, he could have made himself look a lot worse. Odds were she didn't realize just how easy he'd been on her for the past few days. Chance allowed himself a small, grim smile. From his point of view he'd been handling her with kid gloves.

But she couldn't be expected to appreciate that fact. Last night she had even accused him of playing cat-and-mouse with her. Well, maybe he had been. At least a little. Chance stifled a groan of frustration and reminded himself that a woman who found herself in bed with her enemy was bound to have a few problems reconciling her emotional surrender. It meant a lot to him that she'd surrendered as much as she had.

Perhaps she needed time.

Or perhaps she needed to have her attention focused on the fact that there was more going on between them than a dangerous liaison between wary opponents.

Chance's fingers drummed one staccato measure on the quilt as he considered various and assorted ways of making Rachel see the reality of what lay ahead between them.

The rain had stopped outside the window, but the morning was dawning dark and cloudy. Another storm was on the way. There would be more rain by evening. Whatever else happened today, he wanted to get his unwelcome houseguests on their way. He had other more important things to do today than entertain the crew sleeping down the hall.

Chance slid his palm along Rachel's hip, enjoying the hand-filling curve of her buttock. When she stirred beneath his touch, this time he didn't try to keep her from waking. He could feel the mounting tension in his body and wanted to release it in the hot, silken depths of her sweet softness. He was aroused and ready, and he'd decided that Rachel had slept long enough.

"Umm. Chance?" Her eyelashes didn't lift, but he could feel the new awareness in her. She moved, stretching in a lazy, sensual way that lifted her breasts against the sheet. Her nipples were clearly outlined against the white fabric.

"Who else were you expecting?" He dropped a kiss on her shoulder, inhaling the scent that was uniquely hers. He was definitely tuned in to that warm, spicy fragrance now. He was rapidly growing convinced that no other woman would ever be able to completely satisfy his sense of smell.

"I thought you were going to go back to your room before dawn." She opened her eyes and smiled uncertainly. She was still bemused by sleep. Her hand settled on his chest, her fingers threading through the dark triangle of hair that covered him there.

"That was the original intent," Chance admitted. "But you wore me out, I guess. I just woke up myself." He lowered the sheet far enough to toy with one rose-tipped breast, and then watched in satisfaction as her nipple tightened. She was so beautifully responsive to him. Chance wondered if she realized it or if she had any real idea just how unique their passion was. It had been easy to tell that first night that her experience with sex in general was quite limited. He hadn't missed the surprised wonder in her eyes when her body had gently convulsed beneath his. And last night the expression in her blue-green gaze had sent a heady rush of power and satisfaction to his head. *He could make her want him.*

"What time is it?" she murmured, sliding her palm down his stomach and then lower to where his early-morning arousal was announcing itself in no uncertain terms. "Oh."

"I have no idea what time it is, and I know what you mean by 'oh.'" He chuckled and lowered his head again to kiss her. "When you have me in this condition, the time of day is just about the last thing on my mind."

"But I didn't do anything."

"Just waking up next to you is apparently all it takes," he told her.

"I'll remember that." There was a sweet, very feminine amusement in the words.

"You do that." He slid a leg between hers and reached down to find the soft warmth that awaited him between her thighs.

There was one perfunctory knock on the door by way of warning.

An instant later it was opened to reveal Melinda, dressed in a pink robe, her hair brushed into an attractive, fluffy shape that was no doubt supposed to imitate a stylish morning tangle.

"Good morning, Rachel," she began in a suspiciously bright tone. "Have you seen Chance? He's not in his room, and I was wondering if . . . Oh, good heavens, there you are, big brother. Fancy meeting you here. Rachel really is an all-purpose housekeeper, isn't she?"

Chance slowly untangled himself from the stunned woman in bed with him and sat up. He made certain the quilt still covered Rachel as he leveled a gaze at Melinda.

"Get the hell out of here, Mindy. Now."

"Certainly, Chance. Now that we all know what a hypocrite you really are, I'll be glad to go. I guess I've proved my point. Your behavior is hardly a model for anyone else, is it? What right have you got to make decisions about my life when your own is not exactly above reproach? Don't you think it's a little tacky to be sleeping with your housekeeper?"

"Mindy," he said with a soft threat.

"Sure, Chance, I'm going. But do you know something? If I were Rachel I'd be furious at you for trying to make me do double duty as a housekeeper. She's a decent person, and she deserves a little more status than that of paid kitchen slave and bed warmer."

Chance started to shove aside the covers, but it proved unnecessary to physically kick Mindy out of the room. She stepped backward into the hall and quickly slammed the door shut.

Chance sank back against the pillow with a muttered oath and uncovered Rachel's pink face. "Sorry about that. I should have locked the door last night."

"Yes," she agreed tightly, "you should have. Better yet, you should have gone back to your own room before dawn."

He frowned at her. "Hey, are you upset? I mean, I know Mindy is guilty of invading our privacy, but she didn't uncover any big secret affair. I don't give a damn who knows you're sleeping with me."

"Well, that's just ducky for you, isn't it?" She sat up and started to crawl over him to get out of bed.

"Wait one solid second, lady." He was suddenly, coldly angry. He caught her around the waist and pinned her against his bare chest.

He had to fight to ignore the feel of her wriggling, nude body against his own hard frame. There were more important things to worry about at the moment. "Whether you want to admit it or not, our being in bed together is a mutual decision. Remember?"

"I remember." Her eyes were very wide and luminous in the soft morning light. There was a wealth of emotion in her gaze, but Chance wasn't at all sure exactly what that emotion was.

"This is not a case of the lord of the manor having his wicked way with the helpless housekeeper," Chance went on with rigid emphasis.

"I know."

"Then what's the big deal about Mindy's little scene a few minutes ago?"

"It's embarrassing, that's all." Rachel tried to slide free of his grasp, but he kept her where she was. "Please let me go, Chance. I've got breakfast to fix for five people this morning."

"Let 'em fix their own breakfasts. You and I are going to hash this out here and now. I thought we got it all out in the open last night. What's with the housekeeper charade this morning?"

She steadied herself on his chest, her fingers digging into his skin as she said tightly, "What role do you want me to play, Chance? Mistress? Frankly, the part of housekeeper has a little more dignity."

He scowled and released her waist to trap her face between his palms. "We're lovers now. There's no need to find any other labels." He kissed her hard, instinctively trying to impress his claim on her once again, just as he had last night. That damn wariness was still there in her eyes in spite of a night of passion. It frustrated him. More than that, it infuriated him. He wasn't certain how to fight it. All he knew was that he had to find a way.

She froze and then started to soften against him. Chance immediately broke off the kiss, hoping he'd made his point. He released her and gave her a proprietary slap on her rear. "Get dressed and fix breakfast if that's what you really want to do this morning."

She scrambled off the bed, and he watched her hurry across the room to pull her robe out of the closet. She looked terrific in the morning light, he thought. He wanted to pull her back down onto the bed and make love to her once more. His body was still hard.

But even as the thought went through his head he heard the footsteps in the hall.

"The line for the bathroom is already forming," Rachel observed with false cheerfulness. "One of these days we'll—I mean you'll—have to get that second bath functioning." She turned away to tie her sash, obviously unnerved by her use of the word "we."

There was hope, Chance told himself as he stood up and reached for his jeans. "You're right," he agreed blandly. "One of these days we'll have to get that second bath up and running." He fastened his jeans and walked out into the hall with total disregard for whoever might see him leaving his housekeeper's bedroom. If the lady had the guts to plot revenge, face blackmailers and go through with grand confession scenes, she could damn well find the guts to admit she was his lover.

In spite of his best efforts lately, Chance *still* was not a very patient man.

AN HOUR LATER Rachel bustled around the kitchen, grateful for the work involved in serving pancakes to five people. The room was filled with a lot of deliberately light conversation as everyone tried to pretend things were no different this morning than they had been last night. But she hadn't missed the knowing look in Melinda's eyes. The younger woman was just waiting for a chance to use her newfound information. In her battle with her brother, she would use anything she could as ammunition.

Rachel could have throttled Chance for his total lack of concern. There he sat at the head of the table, discussing with Roarke the removal of the tree across the road, paying absolutely no attention to his conniving sister, his anxious mother or his annoyed housekeeper.

It was clear Chance had meant it when he said he didn't give a damn who knew he was sleeping with Rachel or what construction was put on the matter. Typical male, Rachel thought resentfully. It wasn't a source of awkwardness or embarrassment for him. The whole thing probably just put another notch in his ego.

She took a deep breath and told herself she wasn't being strictly fair to Chance. Last night she had wanted him just as much as he had wanted her. But she knew she would have regarded Melinda's invasion with far more equanimity if she had felt secure in her relationship with Chance. If she was sure of his feelings for her, she wouldn't have cared who knew about the affair that had blazed into life between them. But as it was, Rachel wasn't at all certain what he was thinking or feeling.

She didn't doubt his passion, couldn't doubt it. But she had to wonder if their making love the first time hadn't been a means of convincing her to tell him her secrets. He'd admitted last night that he'd known she was hiding something. And as for last night's love-making, it could easily have been a very subtle, thoroughly masculine form of retaliation for the deception and revenge she had originally planned to take.

Except that Chance wasn't exactly a subtle man.

It was all very complicated. Somehow serving thirty pancakes helped take her mind off it.

"You know, Chance," Roarke remarked as he dug into his second pile of pancakes, "I was thinking while I waited for Mindy to free up the shower this morning, I could take a look at the plumbing in your second bath before I leave today. My dad is a plumber. Still runs his own business, and he's taught me a lot. I could probably tell you what's going to have to be done. Interested?"

Chance gave the younger man a considering glance. "All right," he said calmly, to everyone's surprise. "I'll take you up on that. After we get the road cleared."

Melinda's face brightened at once. "Then we'll be staying another night."

Beth winced. "I have to get back home, dear. I had to disrupt my schedule too much as it was to accompany you on this trip. I don't want to spend any more time at Snowball's Chance."

"That's no problem," Melinda said easily. "You take the car and go home. I'll ride back with Roarke tomorrow or the next day."

"You," Chance informed her coolly, "will return with Beth."

Melinda glared at him. "Kicking me out, big brother? I suppose you want some privacy in which to conduct your little affair with the housekeeper."

There was a moment of taut silence around the table, and then Roarke started to say something harsh. Chance waved him aside and turned to his sister.

"As a matter of fact," he said calmly, "I was worried about the baby. I wouldn't want you to take any chances, and I'm sure Roarke wouldn't, either."

A shocked expression crossed Beth's features. Her gaze swung instantly to Rachel. "What baby?"

"Mindy's, of course," Chance murmured dryly as he poured syrup over the remainder of his pancakes. "Hasn't she mentioned she's expecting one? Sorry, didn't mean to spoil the surprise. When's it due, Mindy?"

Melinda's cheeks were turning red with fury and chagrin. Roarke was staring at her as if he'd never seen her before.

"What is this about a baby?" Roarke demanded.

Melinda's flush intensified as she shot a glowering look at her brother. "Nothing," she said petulantly.

Chance smiled evilly. "She arrived yesterday and told me she had to have control of her trust fund because you and she were expecting a child and had to get married. I take it this is news to you?"

"You can say that again," Roarke growled. He put down his knife and fork. "If she's pregnant, it's not by me. I've told Mindy there won't be any talk of marriage and kids until after I've got my doctorate and a job and after she's got her degree. That's final."

"Stop looking at me like that. I'm not pregnant," Melinda cried. "I was just trying to force Chance to be reasonable about my money."

"You know something," Roarke said thoughtfully, "I think Chance is absolutely right. You're not grown up enough to handle your trust fund. I agreed to come up here because I thought you had a right to your own money, and I was willing to help you talk Chance into treating you like an adult. But you're not an adult. You're still acting as if you were nine years old. Run along home, little girl. Call me when you grow up." He tossed his napkin on the table and got to his feet. "I'm going to go outside and take a look at that tree," he informed Chance. "I don't want Mindy to have any excuse to hang around here any longer than necessary."

"I'll be right out to join you," Chance said dryly.

Melinda burst into tears as Roarke stalked out of the kitchen. "Look what you've done, Chance. I told you not to tell anyone about the baby. He hates me now. It's so unfair. It's all so unfair."

"Did you really think I'd let you get away with another nasty crack about Rachel?" Chance asked. "You should know me better than that, Mindy. I put up with a lot from you, but I won't allow you to take pot shots at Rachel. Ever."

Melinda jumped to her feet. "You knew all along there was no baby, didn't you?"

"I've learned to recognize your tearful little games, Mindy."

"But you went ahead and mentioned the baby in front of Roarke and Mom just to punish me!"

"Think of it as justice." He got to his feet and started toward the door. "I'm not the type who gets mad, Mindy. I just get even." He walked out into the hall and disappeared.

Beth got to her feet. "Come along, Mindy. Let's get packed. I think you've managed to wear out your welcome here." She turned to Rachel. "I'm so glad Chance has finally found himself a good woman. That man has been roaming free far too long. Always traveling, never having a home of his own. But I think he's ready to settle down now. His decision to redo Snowball's Chance told me he was starting to get the nesting instinct. Finding you here assures me that it's for real." She smiled warmly. "I look forward to welcoming you into the family. Please don't judge us all by Mindy."

"Mother!" Melinda sobbed more furiously than ever, and ran from the room. "Nobody understands me."

Beth sighed and shook her head. "I keep telling myself that one of these days she really is going to grow up. Maybe I'm deluding myself. Goodbye, Rachel. Take care of Chance. He needs someone to love him. He's been alone much too long."

It was Rachel's turn to shake her head. "I'm not sure he wants someone to love him, Beth. He's a very self-contained man."

"No man is complete without a woman. The truth is women can do much better without a man than vice versa. Deep down I think Chance is smart enough to know he needs you." Beth grinned suddenly. "In any event, he's certainly bright enough to know he wants you."

Rachel groaned. "This is so embarrassing."

"Don't be embarrassed," Beth advised. "Unfortunately, subtlety is not one of Chance's strong points. He tends to be very blunt about what he wants. Very upfront and very assertive. The man was not blessed with any excess patience. Take care, dear. I trust we'll see you again soon. I promise to keep Mindy out of your way."

"Thanks," Rachel said wryly. "I'd appreciate that."

Beth and a very sullen, sulky Melinda were on their way less than an hour later, after Chance and Roarke had rigged up a crude pulley system and succeeded in dragging the downed tree off to the side of the road.

The two men seemed to be on good terms with each other now that Melinda was gone, Rachel decided later as she hung out another load of laundry. Half an hour earlier Chance had taken Roarke up on his offer to have a look at the plumbing in the second bath, and neither man had reappeared.

Rachel grew increasingly anxious as time passed. She wanted to talk to Chance again, but so far there had been no opportunity. She was left to gnaw on her own nerves until lunchtime. When both men eventually appeared for the meal, they spent the whole time talking about plans for plumbing repairs. Finally, around one o'clock Roarke announced his departure.

"Sorry about Mindy," he said to Rachel. "She's a nice kid in a lot of ways, but she has some growing up to do."

Rachel smiled and nodded.

"Rachel understands," Chance said easily. "She's got a younger sister of her own who's at the same retarded stage of social development." He stuck out his hand, and Roarke took it. "Thanks for the plumbing analysis. Now I know what to expect when I tackle that bathroom. I owe you one."

"Forget it. Think of it as repayment for the trouble Mindy and I put you through during the past twenty-four hours." Roarke waved and sauntered out to his car.

Rachel stood on the porch beside Chance and watched Roarke drive off down the road. "He's very nice, Chance."

"Yeah. Too good for Mindy, if you ask me."

Rachel smiled. "She'll mature one of these days."

"Maybe." He sounded skeptical. He glanced at his watch and abruptly swung around and started back into the house. "I'd better get going. I've got some business to handle this afternoon."

"Business!" Rachel hurried after him. "But I thought we could talk, Chance. We have a lot to discuss."

"Did you want to talk about us?" He gave her an unreadable glance as he pocketed his keys.

"Well, yes." Rachel didn't know what else to say. He certainly didn't look particularly enthusiastic. "And about my sister's situation," she added uncertainly, deciding that was a more neutral topic in some ways.

"Don't worry about your sister." He checked his wallet and started for the door. "I'll handle that for you."

"You meant what you said last night? That you'll help prove she wasn't guilty of selling those company secrets?" Rachel was running after him again as he strode outside onto the porch. He was heading for his car.

"I said I'll take care of it, and I will." He opened the door of the vehicle and turned to look at Rachel. "I'll have to break her version of the story first before I can do anything, but I should be able to do that now that I've got you for ammunition. She can't hold out against both of us. Handling your sister should be a piece of cake after what I've just been through with Mindy."

"Thank you," Rachel said humbly. "I think." She stepped back as he got into the vehicle. Then she frowned. "Where are you going?"

"To see Braxton," he replied casually.

"Braxton!" Thoroughly alarmed, Rachel grabbed the edge of the car door and peered through the open window. "What are you going to do with him?"

"I'm going to get rid of him. The man's a pest." Chance twisted the key in the ignition.

"But Chance . . ."

He looked at her. "Forget Braxton. There's something else I want you to worry about while I'm gone."

"But Chance . . ."

He shushed her with an impatient wave of his hand. "I've decided you need to clarify some things in your own mind. So I'm going to help you. We've fooled around long enough, it's time to get everything out in the open."

"But Chance . . ."

"I want you to think twice about whether you should be here when I get back."

Rachel felt suddenly weak at the knees. She gazed at him in mute shock.

Chance paid no attention to the anxiety in her eyes. "If you're here when I get back, I'm going to take that as evidence that you want me and that you intend to make a commitment to our relationship. If you're gone, I'll know you want out. If you do want out, take this opportunity to run, Rachel, because I'm not going to give you another one."

"But Chance . . ." She was stunned.

"And whatever you do, don't let your sister's situation influence you. I gave you my word I'll do what I

can for her and I will, regardless of the situation between you and me. Believe me?"

"I believe you, but, Chance, please wait. We have to
talk about this. I don't understand what you're trying
to do," Rachel gasped.

"Sure you do. I'm trying to force you to figure out
exactly how you feel about me."

"But how do you feel about me?"

"I'll tell you when I get back. If you're still here. Make
your decision, Rachel. I'm tired of trying to figure you
out. I want to know we're involved in a love affair, not
a coy little game." He put the car in gear and spun the
wheel. "Christ, I hate games."

"But Chance…" Rachel was forced to jump back out
of the way as the vehicle roared out of the muddy drive.
She was left standing alone, angry and confused.

They weren't ready for such decisions, she told herself furiously. Their relationship was still finding its
footing. He had no right to give her ultimatums and
force her to make a choice. She wasn't even sure about
his feelings toward her. How could she be expected to
make a decision about this strange relationship when
she wasn't at all certain of his emotions?

There was just too much going on between the two
of them. She couldn't possibly sort it all out so quickly.

This could be a continuation of the retaliation she
had suspected he was meting out by making love to her.
Earlier that morning he had reminded his sister that he
didn't get mad, he got even. On the other hand, Beth

had warned her that Chance was not a particularly subtle man, and that was a fact.

Rachel rubbed her arms in a gesture of indecision and sheer nervous anxiety as she walked slowly back toward the porch. Indecision and anxiety both were states of mind she'd had very little experience with in the past.

If Chance's idea of punishment was the combination of passion and tenderness he had demonstrated toward her last night, than the man was subtle, indeed. Too subtle for the man he was. Too much of a paradox. He wouldn't be able to make love to a woman the way he had to Rachel if he was trying to hurt or punish her. He was incapable of such a cruelly exquisite level of violence. He had too much pride for that sort of thing.

Rachel thought about the previous night, and the confusion and uncertainty she had been experiencing since Melinda had opened the bedroom door finally began to dissipate.

It was true, Rachel thought. She had no way of knowing if Chance might eventually fall in love with her. But she couldn't doubt the reality of the relationship. Chance was a fundamentally honest man, a man of integrity. She believed him, for example, when he said he would help Gail regardless of Rachel's personal decision today.

Therefore she would choose to believe him when he said he wanted a love affair with her.

She loved him too much not to take the risk.

10

THE RAIN THAT HAD BEEN THREATENING all day finally began to fall that afternoon as Chance drove back to Snowball's Chance after the confrontation with Keith Braxton. The stuff would soon be sleeting down, driven by a fitful wind. This storm was going to be a major one.

It crossed Chance's mind that he was already looking forward to starting a fire and sprawling in front of it with a glass of Scotch in his hand and Rachel by his side.

He yanked himself back to reality by reminding himself there was absolutely no guarantee she would be waiting for him when he got home. He had to prepare himself for the possibility that she'd taken him at his word and left, knowing he would keep his promise regarding her sister. Rachel was an independent female. She wouldn't take well to being pushed into such a sudden decision about something as important as a love affair, a love affair with a man who still inspired wariness and caution deep within her. After all, he had until very recently been her enemy.

He probably shouldn't have pushed her so hard this afternoon, Chance thought as he slowed for a sharp curve. It was undoubtedly too soon to start pressuring her in that area. He was already pressuring her enough in other areas of her life.

He might not have done it if she hadn't acted so humiliated about being caught in bed with him that morning. That had annoyed him. He could understand feminine modesty, and he would have forgiven a little embarrassment on her part, but her reaction had gone beyond that in his estimation. Damn it, she had behaved as if she really were just his housekeeper performing a few services on the side for the head of the house.

They were lovers, and he wanted Rachel to accept it and admit it, not try to hide behind a facade.

On the other hand, he admitted, there was no denying the fact that for the past several days she actually had been functioning as his housekeeper. And there had been times when he'd gone out of his way to reinforce the image.

Chance groaned, thinking of the occasions when he'd given her orders and set down rules and regulations. Well, by God, she had been a real housekeeper then. At least he'd been under the impression that she'd signed on for the duration, even if she'd had her own reasons for taking the job.

It was all very complicated, but one thing was clear to Chance as he made his way back to his mountain stronghold. The one surefire way to uncomplicate matters was to get Rachel to admit she was involved with him in a full-blown love affair. He would take care of it from there.

Just as he'd taken care of Keith Braxton.

That last thought brought the ghost of a smile to Chance's stark face. Braxton had crumpled more easily than he'd expected. Mentally Chance reran the scene that had just taken place in Braxton's motel room.

The astonishment on the man's face when he'd opened the door to Chance's knock had provided some satisfaction. Braxton had recovered with commendable quickness, instantly switching on the open-faced, nice-guy image when Chance had laconically introduced himself.

"I'm Chance."

"Mr. Chance! I didn't know you were going to drop by. I take it you've decided to cooperate in an interview, after all? You won't regret it. This is going to be dynamite publicity for you, and now that you're thinking of setting up your own firm, you can use the good press."

"If I need the press, I'll get it somewhere else, Braxton. I don't think giving an interview to a piece of slime will do me much good, do you?" Chance had moved into the room before Braxton could issue an invitation. He had kept his voice soft as he closed the door behind him and locked it. Braxton's eyes had flown to the lock and then back to Chance's emotionless gaze.

"Hey, what's this all about? Are you threatening me? Because if so, you'd better keep in mind that I'm in a position to do you a lot of damage if I choose."

"Braxton, we both know you aren't in a position to do anything more than nip around my heels. And if you get sufficiently annoying all I'll have to do is kick the stuffing out of you. I'm not here about the article you planned to write. Without some cooperation from me, you won't be able to write anything any major magazine editor will be willing to publish. And believe me, a few smears in a tabloid won't even be noticeable."

"You're here because of what that conniving little housekeeper told you, aren't you?"

Chance had lounged back against the door, one thumb hooked in his belt as he regarded the younger man. "That conniving little housekeeper happens to be the lady I'm going to marry."

Braxton's eyes had widened in amazement. "The hell she is! Do you know who she is?"

"Sure. She's Gail Vaughan's stepsister, and she wants to see justice done. I agree with her. Gail took a bad rap at Truett & Tully, and I'll set the record straight. That's not your problem, though. Your only concern, Braxton, is getting out of my sight as fast as you can." Chance had come away from the door without warning, catching the other man by the front of his shirt. "And if you ever bother my woman again I will take you apart into little, tiny pieces. Do you understand me?"

"You can't hurt me," Braxton had sputtered. "I'll have the law on you so fast you won't know what hit you."

Chance had allowed himself a thin smile. "Is that right?"

"Damn right!"

"Then I guess you don't really comprehend just how serious I am about this. Let me make myself clearer. I know why you were fired from that last newspaper you worked for, Braxton. I know all about how you faked that story on the so-called low-income housing scandal, and I also know it wasn't the first story you conjured up out of thin air. There's not a newspaper on the West Coast that will hire you now, is there?"

Braxton's blustering self-confidence had begun to dissolve rapidly at that point. "How do you know about all that? How did you find out?"

"I'm supposed to be a reasonably good investigator, remember? I looked into your background a month ago when you first phoned me about doing the article. I didn't have to look very far to turn up the sleaze. It hung around you like a bad smell. You're washed up as a newspaperman, so now you're trying your hand at freelance writing. But don't hold your breath waiting for your first story to appear. It will be a simple matter for me to make sure every magazine editor knows what every newspaper publisher already knows. You're a liar, and worse, you're a lousy journalist. Even if the publishers were willing to overlook those small details, they won't want to risk the lawsuits you invite."

"This is all that stupid, lying bitch's fault!"

Chance had lost his patience at that point. He had backhanded Braxton with a quick, sure ferocity that had sent the man reeling onto the floor. The last of Braxton's belligerence had disappeared. He had, in fact, become a model of reasonableness shortly thereafter.

Thinking about the matter now, Chance decided everything was under control in that department. Braxton might still manage to put together a sleazy story, but Chance could make certain it didn't get published in any reputable rag. But Braxton wouldn't be writing that story, Chance was sure. Chance had known by the expression in the other man's eyes that Braxton had believed him in the end. If necessary, Chance would take revenge on a very personal basis.

The first bolt of lightning flashed in the hills to his left as Chance neared the turnoff to Snowball's Chance. It was only four o'clock, but the sky was rapidly darkening. The thought of the fire and Rachel and the Scotch made Chance increase his speed slightly.

It was as he came out of a narrow turn that the other car appeared in the rearview mirror, hurtling up behind him. In the blink of an eye, Chance registered the fact that the other car was moving far too fast and that its outside wheel was straying over the white line. The fool was going to pass on a blind curve.

In those last gut-wrenching seconds he realized instinctively what was going to happen. The dark vehicle flashed past him, cutting in much too soon. But

Chance was already braking, his hands clamped around the wheel in an iron grip. He was prepared for the grinding sound of metal as the other car's rear bumper glanced off the front end.

He also knew that if he hadn't slammed on the brake and kept his car rock-steady in its lane, he would even now be airborne over the edge of the cliff on the right-hand side of the road.

It was all over in a heartbeat. The other driver apparently came to his senses a fraction of a second too late. He overcorrected, causing the tail end of his vehicle to swing wide again. He barely managed to keep himself from going over the edge. Then he was gone, engine roaring as the car was gunned out of sight around the next curve.

Chance brought his car to a shuddering halt and then decided that he and the vehicle were still in one piece. A cold anger washed through him. If he moved quickly he could catch the hit-and-run jerk.

He was slamming the car into gear when he heard the distinctive hissing of a tire going flat. So much for his opportunity to administer a dose of citizen justice.

With a short, succinct comment on the subject of reckless drivers, Chance guided his limping car to the edge of the road. The rain broke just as he switched off the ignition.

He sat quietly in the front seat for a moment thinking about coincidences in general and the two that he'd experienced recently. The simple facts were that if he hadn't heard or sensed something at the last possible instant in the coach house the other day, he would have received the full weight of the old radiator on his head instead of just a glancing blow.

And if he had been a fraction slower in reacting he would be at the bottom of a cliff now.

His fingers did a quick, short drumroll on the steering wheel, and then he shoved open the car door. At some point, he told himself wryly, even an unemployed investigator had to start wondering if something odd was going on.

He opened the trunk and hauled out the jack and set to work in the pouring rain. He was suddenly very intent on getting back to Snowball's Chance as fast as possible. For the first time since he'd issued his ultimatum to Rachel, he began to hope she actually had left the house to return to San Francisco.

It tore at his guts to think of her leaving him, but the thought of her being alone in that isolated house right now did even worse things to his insides.

RACHEL PAUSED in front of the cracked mirror in her bedroom and studied herself with a critical eye. She held a coral lipstick poised in one hand. She didn't want to put on too much makeup. That would look too obvious. The fact that she was still here at Snowball's Chance should tell Chance everything he needed to know. By all accounts the man was not *that* slow-witted.

He had given her virtually the same blunt ultimatum his great-great-grandfather had given his wife, Rachel reflected ruefully. And both Rachel and the unknown Mrs. Chance of a previous generation had chosen to take a Chance. Rachel smiled briefly. Standing there in the bedroom that had once belonged to the other woman, she felt a strange sense of kinship with Chance's great-great-grandmother.

She set down the lipstick and went to the closet. The vest and trousers she had worn the day of her arrival would do for this evening. It wasn't as if there was a lot of choice. They were the nicest things she had here at Snowball's Chance.

The fragrance of the coq au vin simmering downstairs wafted up the hallway and through the door of the bedroom. Rachel had invested a lot of time in the dish. She hoped her so-called employer would appreciate it.

Then she started worrying that he might think she was staying in an effort to repay him for his promise to help her sister. Nothing could be further from the truth.

Thoughts of Gail conjured up thoughts of Melinda. As she dressed, Rachel thought briefly that the two young women had far too much in common. Chance was right. They were both spoiled, had an annoying tendency toward melodrama and were not above whining tearfully when they didn't get their own way.

Rachel wondered how many more similarities there were between the two women. Melinda had enacted her latest scene because of a man; it made Rachel wonder for the first time if there was a man involved somewhere in the mess that had blown up around Gail.

Gail had claimed there was one, namely Chance. But Chance had not seduced or framed her. Rachel was certain of that.

And before the whole sordid affair had begun at Truett & Tully, the only man Gail had mentioned was her boss, Ed Fraley. She had talked about him a great deal in recent months.

But how would Fraley or anyone else figure in this mess?

Unless Gail was protecting someone.

Rachel thought of the elaborate charade Melinda Chance had recently conducted in an effort to obtain control over her money so that she could convince Roarke to marry her. Rachel found herself wondering for the first time just how far Gail would go for a man she wanted. A woman caught up in the throes of passion wasn't always rational. All Rachel had to do was take a close look at herself to see that bit of wisdom in action.

The faint squeak at the bottom of the stairs was barely audible over the noise of the rain beating against the window. But something made Rachel pause and listen.

There was no further sound, and she made a face at herself in the mirror. Snowball's Chance seemed very large and very empty this afternoon. Heaven knew it was full of squeaks and stray creaks. She wasn't about to let her imagination get the best of her while she waited for Chance's return.

She glanced at the clock and frowned, wondering what was keeping him. Surely he'd had plenty of time to deal with Braxton. But perhaps Braxton had turned nasty. The thought made her uneasy. Braxton was a snake. There was no telling what he might do when Chance confronted him.

A faint but distinctive creak sounded once again from the staircase. This time Rachel froze. Her nerve endings were tingling. It took her a few seconds to identify the sensation.

It was dread. That weird, creeping sense of dread that came when a woman knew she was no longer alone in a house that was supposed to be empty.

She was suddenly trembling with fear. She told herself it had no logical basis, but the primitive core of her being refused to buy that. Her mind was screaming at her that someone else was in the house.

Rachel forced herself to cross the room to the door. The only way to fight this was to go out into the hall and look at the empty staircase.

She got as far as the door, but when she started to step out into the hall the clamoring of her jangled nerves forbade the movement.

Hide. Run and hide. Her fingers were clamped around the glass doorknob. Her palms were damp. *The closet. Anywhere. Just hide.*

There was silence from the hallway. Too much silence.

Rachel took a deep breath, fighting for rationality and self-control. There couldn't be anyone out there. She hadn't heard a car in the drive. Chance hadn't returned from his meeting with Braxton.

There couldn't be anyone else in the house.

But all her instincts told her there was. Instead of forcing herself out into the hall, Rachel gave in to the silent shouts of warning in her head. She slammed the door shut and locked it.

Instantly there were footsteps, running footsteps coming up the stairs and into the hall.

Rachel's stomach tightened with panic. There was no sense trying to hide in the closet or anywhere else in the room. That was a useless, totally hysterical reaction; she wouldn't succumb to it. She had to think.

She had to get out of here. The bedroom was a trap. She dashed to the French window and yanked it open. The sagging balcony loomed in front of her.

The footsteps came to a halt outside her bedroom door, and somebody tried the knob, jerking it savagely.

Rachel hesitated no longer. She stepped out into the rain, praying that the weakened balcony would hold her weight. Behind her the doorknob rattled violently.

The balcony groaned and creaked beneath her feet, but it held. Cautiously Rachel worked her way to the far end and looked below. She had to get onto the porch roof beneath her. It was her only hope of escape.

The rain poured down on her, plastering her hair and soaking her clothes as she climbed over the railing and dangled for a few tension-filled seconds above the porch. It was farther down to the porch roof than she'd realized.

Then the railing began to give way under her grip. There was no more time to consider the matter. Rachel let go just as the wood snapped under her fingers.

She landed with considerable force on top of the old roof. Thank God Chance had finished repairing it soon after she'd arrived, Rachel thought. She steadied herself and then started for the edge of the roof. She glanced back, just once, at the French windows but saw no one. The old lock on the door was holding. Chance was right, Snowball's Chance was a solidly built place. Good hardware, at any rate.

She was going to feel like an utter fool if whoever was inside the house was simply a friend of Chance's who thought he or she was about to corner a burglar.

But any visitor would have arrived openly by car. Whoever had come up those stairs had been an intruder. Possibly a dangerous vagrant seeking shelter from the storm.

Rachel glanced longingly at her car as she scrambled over the edge of the roof and sought for footing on the railing below. Her keys were where they always were, in her purse, which was sitting in a drawer in the hall.

They might as well have been in Siberia for all the good they did her.

She would have to run for it. Her best bet was the road. She might get lucky and meet Chance returning from town. But if whoever was inside the house followed her, he might easily be able to outrun her. He might have a gun.

Rachel's polished leather loafers slipped on the wet wood of the porch railing, and she tumbled ignominiously down into the bushes, which cushioned her fall.

Stifling a scream, she picked herself up and dashed instinctively for the nearest shelter, the coach house.

The first shot came a split second ahead of a roll of thunder. Rachel wasn't even certain there had been a gunshot. The mechanical noise blended with the natural roar of nature.

Rachel kept running.

A few seconds later she careered through the door of the coach house. She slammed it shut behind her, breathing hard, and found herself gazing into the gloom of the darkened building.

The light, she thought, automatically reaching for the switch. No, light was a bad idea. Her eyes would adjust soon, and she might have some minimal advantage over the intruder if he chose to follow her into the building. Of course that advantage would vanish as soon as the intruder found the wall switch.

Then she heard the sound of the car in the drive.

Chance. It had to be Chance.

Whirling, Rachel yanked open the door, standing to one side so that no one could see her from the bedroom window. Chance's vehicle came to a halt a few feet away. The car door opened, and he started to get out.

"Chance! Over here. I'm over here."

He turned his head and saw her. "Rachel? What the hell . . . ?"

"There's someone in the house. I think he's got a gun!" she yelled back. "Be careful."

But Chance was already moving, racing toward her in a tight crouch that made him a difficult target. A shot cracked in the rain just as he made it through the door-way and spun around to close the door. He grabbed Rachel's arm and pulled her away from the door.

"Get away from there. Are you all right?" His smoky eyes glittered with savage intent as he looked down at her.

"I'm okay, Chance. I heard him coming up the stairs, and I went out through the balcony window."

"Oh, Christ. You're damn lucky the balcony held. Tell me fast. What's going on?" Chance was already yanking Rachel through the maze of old equipment and rusting tools toward the wooden ladder that led to the loft. "Who is it in the house?"

"I don't know. Maybe some criminal type who thought the place was empty and would make a good shelter from the storm?"

"Or maybe someone who likes to drop radiators on people's heads and run cars off mountain roads."

"What are you talking about?" Rachel looked at him in horror, trying to see him through the gloom.

"I'll tell you later." He pushed her ahead of him up the ladder. "Hurry, Rachel."

"Are you going to tell me what the big plan is, or do I get to guess?" She clung to the ladder rails as she scurried up ahead of him.

"I've been telling you all along that the junk in this place was good for something." Chance was busying himself with the light bulb that hung from the ceiling. He was removing it. Now there was no source of light within the coach house that could be switched on by an intruder. She shivered at the implications. There was just barely enough gray light seeping through the cracks in the walls for her to make out the shapes of the bulkiest objects surrounding her. Fortunately Chance knew his way around the collection of junk. He should, she thought grimly. He'd certainly spent enough time in here sorting out all the "good stuff."

"Okay, I give up. What is this junk good for?" she demanded as he vaulted up the ladder to the floor of the loft, where she was crouching between two old mattresses and a trunk full of crumbling newspapers.

"I'm not sure yet," Chance admitted, "but I'm sure I'll think of something. I usually do." He peered into the shadows, reaching out to thump the mattresses. "Take these, for instance. You wanted me to cart these off to the dump, remember?"

"I remember. Chance, don't tease me. What are we going to do?"

"We're going to prepare a trap. Give me a hand, woman. We probably don't have much time. Whoever's out there is aware we're not armed, and he must have seen us dash in here. He'll be along any minute."

"I was afraid of that." Rachel got to her feet and banged her head against the rafter. "Ouch. Damn it."

"Watch your head," Chance said absently as he pushed the mattresses toward the edge of the loft.

"Yeah, right," Rachel muttered. She wrinkled her nose at the musty smell of the old cotton ticking.

When the mattresses were in position, they stood them upright, and Chance balanced them in place with one hand while he looked at Rachel. "All right, now hold these here while I get a few more things ready."

"You really think he'll come in here?" Rachel whispered as she watched him line up an assortment of other potential missiles and bombs along the edge of the loft.

"Unless he decides to steal your car instead. If we hear the engine, we'll know whoever it is decided to split and leave us in peace."

"But if we don't hear an engine, we have to assume the worst, huh?"

"Let's just say we're going to have a contingency plan ready."

They heard the coach house doorknob rattle just as Chance moved a length of lead pipe into position. He went still and signaled Rachel to remain motionless behind the upright mattresses.

Her eyes fixed on Chance's profile as he crouched nearby. In the gloom it would be impossible for the intruder to see them up here in the loft, unless they moved or leaned over the edge.

Rachel heard the door open. A shaft of weak, cloudy light from outside gave some illumination to the downstairs portion of the coach house but did nothing to reveal the upper reaches. She held her breath and waited for the signal from Chance.

The stranger's voice, when he spoke, was taut with urgency and nervous tension.

"You might as well come out," the man rasped. "I know you're in here. Both of you. And I know you don't have a gun. *Come out where I can see you.*"

When there was no movement or response from his victims, the intruder grew bolder. Or perhaps he was just getting desperate, Rachel thought. Something in his voice suggested he was as unsettled and nervous as she was, and that astonished her. Surely criminals were cooler customers than this.

"I've got the gun here," the man snarled. "You have to come out. I'm giving the orders now. Move. Where are you, damn it?"

Rachel could tell from the sound of his voice that he'd walked farther into the building. She kept her eyes on Chance's still, crouched form.

"Where are you?" The man's voice rose, rapidly approaching hysteria.

Rachel heard his footsteps down below and knew he was almost directly under the mattresses she was balancing. She swallowed and found her mouth very dry. *Now,* she thought, *it has to be now. We won't get a better opportunity, and besides, if we wait any longer I'll go nuts.*

As if he'd read her mind, Chance shifted silently in the shadows. He came closer to her, touching her hand briefly in a small but definite signal.

Together they shoved the heavy, rotten mattresses over the edge of the loft floor.

There was an instant of silence, and then a startled shout that was almost immediately muffled as the mattresses landed squarely on the intruder.

Chance didn't wait for the results. He was already halfway down the ladder, a rusty old wrench stuck through his belt like a saber. As he leaped down the iron rungs into the gray light below, Rachel thought he looked like a pirate going over the side of his ship to board an enemy vessel.

Rachel leaned over the edge of the loft, able to see what was happening because of the weak light pouring through the open door. There was no sign of the gunman, but his location was obvious from the frantic movements under the mattresses.

Chance was on him in a moment, wrench in hand. He shoved aside the thick, heavy mattresses and kicked the dropped gun out of reach. The intruder was sprawled on his back on the dusty floor, staring in resentful fury at the man who stood over him.

"Damn you, Chance. You've got more luck than any man has a right to claim. *Damn you.*"

"I like to think it's more than luck," Chance said dryly. "But you may be right."

Rachel stared down at the two men. "Chance? Who is it? Do you know him?"

"Sure, I know him. And so does Gail. Meet Ed Fraley, a hotshot manager at Truett & Tully. Gail used to be his private secretary."

"Fraley? Her boss?" Rachel was shocked. Then a grim sense of foreboding swept over her as she examined the good-looking man lying at Chance's feet. Blond hair, good physique and the looks of a currently popular television star. This was just the sort of man Gail might have chosen to fall in love with. The kind of man for whom she might have made a very big mistake in the name of passion. "Good grief, Chance, what do you think is going on here?"

"I think," Chance said calmly as he reached down to yank Fraley to his feet, "that Fraley is the one who was selling secrets at Truett & Tully. And I think your foolish sister was silly enough to believe herself in love with him. So much in love that when he planted the evidence against her, she took the blame rather than point the finger at her boss. How about it, Fraley? Is that what happened?"

Fraley glowered at Chance as he struggled to his feet. He said sullenly, "I knew you didn't completely buy Gail as the thief. I knew it the day your boss pulled you off the case and declared it closed. You were madder than hell, kept arguing that it wasn't that simple. And you have a reputation for not giving up until you've got all the answers. I was afraid you might eventually convince Dixon Security and my firm to reopen the case. The more I thought about it, the more I realized I had to do something. I couldn't take any risks. The set-up was too good."

"So you decided to find me and arrange a convenient accident. It probably sounded simple enough in the beginning. But things started going wrong. The radiator didn't work, because I managed to dodge at the last possible second. I must have heard you heaving it over the edge of the loft. You thought I was dead, didn't you? All the blood from the gash on my head. It would have fooled you. And I was badly dazed for several minutes afterward. I wasn't aware of anything, not even of you dashing out of here. Then you tried sideswiping me on the road this afternoon, but that didn't work, either. You're better at corporate crime than the more physical kind. You obviously haven't had much practice with the rough stuff. But this afternoon, after you failed to shove my car over the edge of the cliff, you panicked."

"He came here looking for you with a gun," Rachel whispered.

Chance nodded, his eyes still on Fraley. "You decided to take drastic action, didn't you, Fraley? You wanted to get this over with, and you were getting very nervous because nothing had worked right yet. What did you expect the cops to think? That Rachel and I had been the victims of a vicious stranger who had wandered in out of the storm? Casual, random violence?"

"It would have worked if that bitch hadn't gone out the window and warned you the way she did. It would have worked!" Fraley's voice rose to an hysterical, sobbing moan. "It should have worked. All of it. I had it all figured out. Damn that stupid little—"

"You know what?" Chance said very softly. "I'm getting sick and tired of hearing people malign the woman I'm going to marry." He slammed a fist into Fraley, and watched with obvious satisfaction as the man crumpled down onto the floor.

"My hero," Rachel murmured.

Chance glanced up at her, seeking her face in the shadows. "Is that right?"

"You bet. Are you really going to marry me?"

"Yeah. I can't seem to think of any other way to keep you out of trouble." He looked down at Fraley again. "I'll have to admit you were right about one thing, Rachel."

"What's that?"

"The male variety of melodramatic whiner-complainer is just as annoying as the female variety. Just as common, too, apparently. This is the second one I've run into today."

"For someone whose patience span is as limited as yours, it's been a hard day."

11

It was a long time before Chance got to sit in front of a roaring fire with a glass of Scotch in his hand and an arm around Rachel.

"If the housekeepers' union could only see me now," Rachel remarked. She had her head resting on Chance's shoulder and her legs curled up under her on the lumpy sofa. Tonight she didn't even mind the lumps.

"Who cares?" Chance said. "You'll be resigning from that gang. They were a demanding bunch, anyway. You'll be joining the wives' union just as soon as I can arrange it."

"I should warn you they run a much stricter, more demanding operation than the housekeepers'. When it comes to contract negotiation time, you'd better be prepared for a fight."

Chance grinned. "I told you I've always had a soft spot for the feisty types. And you're about as feisty as they come, Rachel, my sweet. Speaking of gutsy behavior, whatever possessed you to exit the bedroom via the balcony this afternoon?"

"It was either that or cower in a closet. Under the circumstances, that didn't make a whole lot of sense."

Chance shook his head in grim wonder. "When I think of what could have happened this afternoon I come unglued somewhere inside. Fraley meant to kill only me in the beginning, but when he came back to the house and found you here, he lost his cool and figured he'd get rid of you, too. He was tired of waiting for another shot at me when I was alone. He decided to make you a victim of the so-called intruder, too."

"Would you have done what Fraley feared you would? Would you have reopened that case at Truett & Tully if I hadn't come along?"

"I probably would have kept after Dixon about it. I was trying to bribe him by telling him I'd go back to work for a few more months if he'd let me have the Truett & Tully case. I think eventually I would have worn him down. I wasn't satisfied with the confession we got from your sister, and he's too good an investigator to have stayed satisfied with it, either. But I had no immediate plans to do much beyond prod Herb. Hell, there wasn't much I could do. Not as long as Gail stuck to her story."

"Fraley was probably right to be nervous about what you might or might not do." Rachel sighed. "It's going to be interesting to see what Gail has to say for herself when I confront her about Fraley."

"She's not the first woman to take the fall for some manipulating man."

"True." Rachel smiled. "Unfortunately, not all males are as unsubtle and straightforward as you are. Some are downright sneaky."

Chance took a swallow of his Scotch. A slow, satisfied smile edged his mouth. "Not all females have the guts to plot revenge and then abandon it for love. I want you to know I was quite touched."

"Hah. I didn't abandon my mission because I fell in love with you."

"No?"

"Absolutely not. I had far more pragmatic reasons," Rachel declared. "I'm not weak in the head, you know."

He patted her on top of her head in an indulgent gesture. "Sure."

"It's true," she emphasized grandly. "I gave up my plans for vengeance for the simple reason that I came to the conclusion you weren't subtle enough to have seduced and framed my sister. It was straight, deductive analysis that made me decide you were probably innocent."

There was a short pause while Chance absorbed that. "I think you may have just insulted me," he finally declared. "What's all this about lacking subtlety? I'll have you know I'm very subtle when the occasion demands."

"You might be subtle in your thinking when you're pulling together the threads of an investigation," Rachel allowed generously.

"Thanks." He grinned wickedly.

"But when it comes to dealing with women, you are not very subtle at all."

"The heck I'm not! What about all those days I spent coaxing you into telling me who you really were?"

"What about them? The project didn't work, did it?" She slanted him a teasing glance from under her lashes. "I told you the truth for good and sufficient reasons. First, I thought you were innocent of framing Gail, and second, I had a blackmailer on my back, and third—" She broke off abruptly.

"Yes?" Chance prodded, eyes gleaming. "What was the last reason?"

Rachel snuggled more closely into his hold. "Because I knew I was in love with you, and I didn't want there to be any more mysteries or misunderstandings between us."

"Which, translated, means I am such a subtle lover, you fell in love with me in spite of all your fears," he concluded.

"Your ego is showing."

"That's okay. I fell in love with you even though I knew there was something phony about the housekeeper story right from the start."

The teasing light went out of Rachel's eyes as she looked up at him with a searching gaze. "Did you really?"

He dropped a soft kiss on her hair. "Really."

She hesitated. "If you were sure this afternoon that you loved me, why did you give me that choice between going back to San Francisco or staying here and waiting for you?"

"At that point I wasn't sure you realized you loved me," he told her honestly. "I wanted you to take a good look at your feelings and accept what was happening between us. It was time you made some decisions. I knew you were still wary of me in some ways."

"Only natural considering the fact that I wasn't sure how you felt about me," she pointed out.

"I wanted a commitment from you."

"And you wanted it now. This instant. The moment you asked for it. No stalling." Rachel shook her head, a trace of wry amusement in her eyes.

"I saw no reason to let you dither any longer about the matter."

"No patience with a woman's indecisiveness, hmm? You see what I mean about your lack of subtlety and finesse?"

He grinned. "I got what I wanted, didn't I? In the end, that's all that counts."

"I'm glad you want me, Chance."

A devil laughed at her from his eyes. "I started wanting you the minute I saw you. But when I realized you were going to dig in and really work here at Snowball's Chance, instead of moan and complain the way Mrs. Vinson did, I was lost. I fell head over heels in love."

"I seem to recall voicing a few complaints along the way. What about the morning I informed you that I wanted hot water for my shower?" she protested.

"You were very straightforward about it. You didn't whine, and you didn't let it stop you from getting any work done," he said magnanimously.

"It's nice to know I'm appreciated for my finer qualities," Rachel observed dryly.

"Oh, you're very definitely appreciated." He nuzzled the area behind her ear as she muttered a soft, exasperated protest, which he ignored. "I'll tell you something, though. This afternoon while I changed that damn tire in the rain, I started hoping you had chosen to go back to San Francisco."

She pulled back to stare at him, her eyes wide and questioning. "Why?"

His smoky gaze darkened. "Because I was finally beginning to put some facts together. I was a little slow on the uptake on this case, I'll grant you that. You have to remember that as far as I was concerned, I was off the case altogether. I had no reason to suspect it had followed me to Snowball's Chance. But this afternoon as I was thinking about the fact that a flight over a cliff wasn't my idea of fun, it occurred to me that two near misses in the span of a few days was a bit much. The car that had just sideswiped me kept going. If someone was after me, I had to allow for the possibility that whoever was inside the car might decide to go to the house and wait for me. His vehicle could have been hidden somewhere alongside the road on any one of a number of little tracks or turnoffs. Then whoever was inside could simply walk to the house on foot, alone and un-

noticed. I realized that if you hadn't gone back to San
Francisco—"

"Which you knew I hadn't," Rachel said staunchly.

He shrugged. "Then you'd be here at Snowball's
Chance cooking my dinner and fixing my Scotch like a
good little housekeeper. You'd be totally vulnerable to
the jerk who had just tried to kill me. I didn't know
whether I had anything to worry about for certain, but
believe me, I've never changed a tire so fast in my life.
I'm probably going to get occasional anxiety attacks for
the next few years thinking about how close it all was."

"Somehow I don't see you suffering an anxiety attack." Rachel put her arms around his neck. "But I'm
glad to know you care." She kissed his throat. "Very,
very glad."

His eyes blazed with a fierce emotion as he set down
his glass and pulled her across his thighs. His arms were
warm and strong around her. "Oh, I definitely care,
Miss Rachel Wilder. I've never cared for or about anything this much in my entire life."

"Love me, Chance."

"Forever," he whispered, and lowered his mouth to
hers.

"RACHEL, STOP TREATING me like a child," Gail wailed
the next day as she confronted her sister and Chance.
"You don't know how it was between me and Ed. You
don't know what it's like to be passionately in love.
You've only ever cared about business and about your
career." Her beautiful hazel eyes, brimming with

unshed tears, went from her sister's calm features to Chance's stark, unrelenting expression. "Neither of you understand. You're both, well, *older*. You don't know what it's like—"

"Spare us the dramatics," Chance interrupted coldly. "And for Pete's sake, stop whining. Just run through the whole thing as quickly as possible, all right? Short, simple sentences with no melodrama. I want to make certain I've cleared up all the details."

"I trusted him," Gail murmured through her unshed tears. She plucked another tissue from the box in her lap. "I knew there was an investigation going on at Truett & Tully, of course. That was no secret at Ed's management level, and anything a manager knows, his secretary knows, too. When I accidentally found some documents he'd hidden in a file and asked him if he knew anything about them, he told me he was helping Dixon Security set a trap for the real thief. He said that since I had discovered what was going on, I was obligated to assist in the investigation."

"So you kept your mouth shut, and the next thing you knew I walked into your office and found those documents." Chance shoved his hands into his back pockets in an impatient, irritated movement. "Why didn't you say something at the time? I asked you point-blank for your side of the story. All you did was cry a lot and say you didn't understand what was happening."

Gail looked as though she were about to lose control of her tears. But when Rachel instinctively started forward to comfort her, Chance gave a small, negative shake of his head. Reluctantly Rachel took a grip on her automatic big-sister emotions. "What happened, Gail?" she prompted gently.

Gail turned to her, seeking comfort from one of the many people in her life who had always offered it. "Ed had warned me that part of the investigation might involve Dixon Security faking a discovery of missing documents in order to put everyone off guard and trap the real thief. Ed said that if it happened, I was to go along with it. When Mr. Chance walked into my office that day and dug out that particular file, I thought that was part of the plan. Then he started pushing me, prodding me, baiting me. He never let up, never stopped making me repeat my story. I didn't understand. I thought I was part of the plan. He just kept after me, and I finally realized I was the one Dixon Security was going to blame. I didn't know what was going on, so as soon as I was alone I went to Ed and asked him what I was supposed to do next."

"What was Fraley's advice?" Chance asked grimly. "Did he tell you to just keep quiet and everything would be all right in the end?"

Gail nodded morosely. "He said things had gone wrong. He claimed Dixon Security was an inept, bungling outfit that just wanted to place the blame somewhere, and it had chosen our office. Ed said that if I didn't claim that I was guilty, you would go after him, and if you got him fired there would be no one left at Truett & Tully to find the real thief. He also said that if he got fired, I would be let go, anyway, because no one would believe I hadn't been involved. It was all so confusing. I didn't know what to do."

Rachel closed her eyes. "So Ed took you out to dinner, knowing you had a crush on him, and asked for your help, right? He told you everything would be all right, that he would find the real thief and get you reinstated. But in the meantime, you were to pretend to be guilty so that the real thief would think everything had blown over."

"I thought he loved me as much as I loved him!"

"Yes, well, he didn't, did he?" Chance's voice lacked even the smallest degree of sympathy. "He just wanted to use you."

Rachel looked at her sister's delicate profile. "You made up that nonsense about Chance having framed you when I began demanding some answers about why you'd lost your job."

"I had to come up with some reason to explain the whole thing, and I couldn't bear to have you think I was guilty of selling those secrets. How was I to know you'd go crazy and track down Mr. Chance?"

"You should have known she'd do something," Chance said bluntly. "It's her nature. Rachel doesn't crumple up into a useless little ball of tissue when things get rough. She takes action. She doesn't waste time bewailing fate, she fights back. In this case she was fighting for you."

"I never asked her to do something about my situation," Gail said with a sob.

"Maybe she felt a certain responsibility to do it, anyhow," Chance pointed out ruthlessly. "After all, she's your sister, and it was fairly obvious you weren't capable of fighting back on your own behalf."

"I thought Ed was going to take care of everything!"

"How long were you going to protect Fraley?" Rachel asked.

Gail's mouth tightened. "He must have known that sooner or later I'd get suspicious and that I'd want to clear my name."

"He wasn't worried about that," Chance said. "Who would believe you? You took the blame at the time, and you were going to keep quiet for a few weeks, maybe months, if he was lucky. By the time you finally decided you'd been had, no one would have cared or listened. Your protests of innocence would have come much too late. But in the meantime, Fraley began to worry about his future. He wasn't concerned about what you might eventually decide to say, but he knew I had a reputation for digging around until I was satisfied. And he suspected I wasn't totally satisfied with the Truett & Tully case. Having me officially pulled off the case didn't give him any peace of mind. The more he thought about it, the more nervous he got. He had a lot at stake. The secrets he was leaking were making him a fortune. He decided to track me down and see that I was taken out of the picture."

"He tried to kill Chance three times," Rachel said, her hands tightening into small fists.

"Fortunately, he was not exactly a professional at that kind of thing," Chance said dryly. "His expertise was in the area of stealing company secrets and seducing silly little secretaries."

"I am not a silly little secretary!" Gail insisted, and the tears began to fall in earnest.

Rachel shot Chance a glowering look and went forward to put her arms around her sister. "It's all right, Gail. We all make mistakes. Especially when we're in love."

"Not you, Rachel," Gail sobbed. "You'd never make the kind of mistake I made. You've never been in love enough to make a really big mistake."

"This is enough to turn a man's stomach," Chance muttered from the other side of the room.

Rachel met his eyes over her sister's bent blond head. "Not another word out of you, Chance, or I'll personally burn that entire collection of 1940s magazines you found in the coach house the other day."

"Did I say anything nasty?" Chance asked blandly. "Go ahead and comfort the poor, innocent victim. I'm going to give Herb Dixon a call." He strode out of the room, whistling tunelessly. At the doorway he paused for an instant and shot a considering look at Rachel. "You know what? I think maybe you and I have been guilty of overprotecting our little sisters. I think it's time we let them find out how the big, bad world really works. They've got to learn to cope someday."

Rachel met his eyes in sudden agreement and understanding. "You may be right," she said seriously.

Chance nodded once, briskly, and went on through the doorway.

Gail lifted her head, sniffling, and looked after him. "He's a hard man, isn't he?"

"Let's just say he doesn't suffer fools gladly. And I don't think he appreciated his role in your little tale of woe. Whatever made you tell me he was the one who had seduced and framed you?"

"I told you, I didn't want you to think I was the thief," Gail said wretchedly. "But I knew you were suspicious about the real reason I'd resigned. I had to think of some story to give you so that you'd know I was innocent, but I couldn't tell you the whole truth. I knew you'd go straight to Truett & Tully management, and Ed had said we had to keep everything secret. So I sort of made up that bit about Chance seducing me." Gail swallowed and blew her nose. "Now that I've gotten to know him a little better, I can see it wasn't a very likely tale, was it? What woman would be dumb enough to get herself seduced by that . . . that cruel, rude, short-tempered, ruthless man?"

"Darned if I know," Rachel said with a small grin.

TWO WEEKS LATER Rachel finished chopping vegetables for dinner, then took off her apron and poured two glasses of Scotch. As she put the bottle away in the cupboard, she glanced out the window at the rapidly darkening sky and decided there was more rain on the way. It would be a cozy night to sit in front of the fire and make plans for the future with her new husband.

But first she had to get Chance out of the coach house and into a shower. He had been busy since three o'clock that afternoon sorting through his priceless collection of junk.

Some honeymoon, she thought with an inner smile. If anyone had told her last month that she would be spending the two weeks following her marriage working on Snowball's Chance, she would have called him crazy. But somehow it was all working out just fine. Somewhere along the line she had become as sentimental about the old house as Chance had. She knew she and Chance would be spending a lot of time here during the years ahead.

Rachel stepped out onto the porch, her hair whipping in the wind that was preceding the storm. She hurried across the yard to the old coach house, thinking about the mad dash she'd made three weeks earlier. The new gold wedding band on her left hand gleamed in the gray twilight.

She reached the door of the coach house and found the overhead light on inside. There was no sign of her husband.

"Chance?"

"I'm up here," he called from the loft.

Rachel headed for the ladder and climbed far enough to be able to peer over the edge of the loft floor. Chance was tugging a stained canvas off a large, unidentifiable shape in the far corner of the loft.

"It's time for a drink and dinner," Rachel informed him. Then she caught sight of some familiar items. "What in the world are those old mattresses doing back up here? You said you were going to throw them away."

"I changed my mind when I started to tie them onto the roof of the car. You never know when something like those mattresses might come in handy," Chance said defensively.

"If you think I or anyone else who ever stays at Snowball's Chance is going to sleep on those tattered, musty old things, you're out of your mind."

"Well, they've got sentimental value. Every time I look at them I'll think of the day you and I declared our love for each other." He smiled winningly.

"Don't give me that. You're saving them because you can't bear to throw anything away, even an old, useless mattress." Rachel laughed at him. "You're impossible, Abraham Chance, do you know that?"

"There's plenty of room here at Snowball's Chance to store a few old mementos."

"Dingy, dusty, moldy old mattresses are hardly world-class mementos." Rachel climbed the rest of the way up the ladder.

"One person's junk is another's treasure," Chance said with lofty disdain. "Hey, take a look at this." He finished removing the canvas with a flourish and revealed his prize.

Rachel stared at the old Victorian couch. It was covered in purple velvet that was surprisingly clean and dust free. The wood of the gracefully curving back and arms was intricately carved, and the feet looked like the clawed paws of some mythical animal.

"Good heavens," Rachel said in wonder as she approached the odd piece of furniture. "A jewel in the attic. Why would anyone hide something like that up here? It's going to look fantastic in the living room."

Chance grinned in satisfaction. "There's hope for you yet. I knew sooner or later I'd come across something you'd want to keep." He sat down on the velvet-covered cushion. It sank a little beneath his weight. "It's in great shape."

Rachel wandered around it, running her hand along the beautifully carved wooden frame. "Amazing. Whoever put it up here certainly wrapped it well. I wonder how long it's been hidden here in the coach house."

"Who knows? Somebody probably stuffed it up here when it went out of style." Chance reached out and snagged her wrist, dragging her down into his lap. He leered at her good-naturedly. "It's in great condition. It's going to do just fine for another generation or so. We might as well use it to get in practice."

Rachel's eyebrows rose. "In practice for what?"

"For making love in the executive suite of Chance Security," he explained as if she were a little slow. "I figure we'll be spending a lot of time on the couch there."

"Hmm. A distinct possibility." Rachel toyed with the buttons of his shirt and tilted her head thoughtfully. "You know, when I went into the field of corporate planning analysis, I never envisioned myself planning for an investigative firm."

"The business is the same as any other corporate enterprise. It needs long-range planning analysts and top-flight executive ability." Chance nuzzled her ear. "I have it on the best authority that you're an expert in that sort of thing."

"Is that why you persuaded me to quit my job and join your new firm?"

"No. I did that because I like to hire gutsy people who aren't afraid to take the bull by the horns and do whatever is necessary to get the job done." His fingers eased under her sweater and found her unconfined breasts. He brushed his fingertip over one nipple. "Speaking of getting the job done . . ."

"What about it?" she asked absently, turning her face into his shoulder. She could feel the strength in him reaching out to enfold her, and it brought her alive as nothing else could. She stirred sensuously in his grasp, and the hand on her breast tightened possessively.

"I think it's time I did my husbandly duty today." Chance's gravel-and-ice voice was deep and husky with arousal.

"You already did your duty this morning. You woke me up to do it, in fact, remember?"

"That was just practice."

"Oh." She shivered as he unsnapped her jeans and stripped them off her hips. "I hadn't realized. I thought it was for real. It certainly felt real."

"You can be a little tease, you know that?" He settled her down onto the couch, shrugging quickly out of his own clothes. "Fortunately I'm a patient, indulgent sort of husband."

Rachel's eyes widened in amazement. "Since when?"

"Since the moment I met you," he assured her. His eyes were brilliant with desire as he lowered himself along the length of her. His body fitted itself to hers with solid power, and Chance groaned with pleasure as he parted Rachel's legs and sheathed himself in her soft, clinging warmth. When she gasped at the impact and clutched at him, his mouth curved in satisfaction. "Have I told you lately that I love you, Mrs. Rachel Wilder Chance?"

"Not since lunch." Rachel wrapped her legs around him. She hugged him close. "You can tell me again, if you feel like it."

He caught her ear between his teeth and nibbled gently. "I love you."

"I love you," she whispered, her heart in her eyes as she lay looking up at him.

Chance moved slowly and deliberately, stroking deeply into her until Rachel caught her breath and closed her eyes. Her fingernails made small marks on his back that caused Chance to mutter other, more intimate words into her ear.

The storm broke outside, but the coach house was dry and comfortable. Like Snowball's Chance itself, it had been built to last.

And just as Chance had predicted, the old Victorian fainting couch proved sturdy enough to serve another generation of Chances.

New York Times Bestselling Author

BARBARA DELINSKY

**Look for her at your favorite retail outlet this
September with**

A SINGLE ROSE

A two-week Caribbean treasure hunt with rugged and
sexy Noah VanBaar wasn't Shaye Burke's usual style.
Stuck with Noah on a beat-up old sloop with no engine,
she was left feeling both challenged and confused. Torn
between passion and self-control, Shaye was afraid of
being swept away by an all-consuming love.

Available in September, wherever Harlequin books are sold.

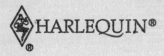

Where do you find hot Texas nights, smooth Texas charm and dangerously sexy cowboys?

Crystal Creek reverberates with the exciting rhythm of Texas.
Each story features the rugged individuals who live and love in the
Lone Star state.

"...Crystal Creek wonderfully evokes the hot days and steamy nights of
a small Texas community...impossible to put down until the last page
is turned."
—*Romantic Times*

"...a series that should hook any romance reader. Outstanding."
—*Rendezvous*

"Altogether, it couldn't be better."   —*Rendezvous*

Don't miss the next book in this exciting series:
LET'S TURN BACK THE YEARS by BARBARA KAYE

Available in August wherever Harlequin books are sold.

HARLEQUIN®
Temptation®
IS TEN!

Join the festivities as Harlequin celebrates
Temptation's tenth anniversary in 1994!

Look for tempting treats from your favorite
Temptation authors all year long. The celebration
begins with Passion's Quest—four exciting sensual
stories featuring the most elemental passions....

The temptation continues with Lost Loves, a sizzling
miniseries about love lost...love found. And watch for
the 500th Temptation in July by bestselling author
Rita Clay Estrada, a seductive story in the vein
of the much-loved tale, THE IVORY KEY.

In May, look for details of an irresistible offer:
three classic Temptation novels by Rita Clay Estrada,
Glenda Sanders and Gina Wilkins in a collector's
hardcover edition—free with proof of purchase!

After ten tempting years, *nobody* can resist

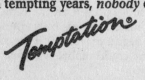

HARLEQUIN®
Temptation

Lost Loves

RIGHT MAN...WRONG TIME

Remember that one man who turned your world upside down. Who made you experience all the ecstatic highs of passion and lows of loss and regret. What if you met him again?

You dared to lose your heart once and had it broken. Dare you love again?

JoAnn Ross, Glenda Sanders, Rita Clay Estrada, Gina Wilkins and Carin Rafferty. Find their stories in Lost Loves, Temptation's newest miniseries, running May to September 1994.

In GOLD AND GLITTER, #501 by Gina Wilkins, Michael Spencer, a down-on-his-luck cowboy and single father, still dreamed of his ex-wife. She'd left him and their child for her country music career, but whenever her songs played on the radio, he couldn't help but remember.... It was only after he met Libby Carter that he began to wonder if he could ever let go of the past. If he could realize what was gold and what was glitter?

What if...?

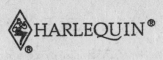

HARLEQUIN®

WEDDING SONG
Vicki Lewis Thompson

Kerry Muldoon has encountered more than her share of happy brides and grooms. She and her band—the Honeymooners—play at all the wedding receptions held in romantic Eternity, Massachusetts!

Kerry longs to walk down the aisle one day— with sexy recording executive Judd Roarke. But Kerry's dreams of singing stardom threaten to tear apart the fragile fabric of their union....

WEDDING SONG, available in August from Temptation, is the third book in Harlequin's new cross-line series, **WEDDINGS, INC.** Be sure to look for the fourth book, **THE WEDDING GAMBLE,** by Muriel Jensen (Harlequin American Romance #549), coming in September.

WED3

HARLEQUIN®

Don't miss these Harlequin favorites by some of our most distinguished authors!
And now you can receive a discount by ordering two or more titles!

HT #25525	THE PERFECT HUSBAND by Kristine Rolofson	$2.99	☐
HT #25554	LOVERS' SECRETS by Glenda Sanders	$2.99	☐
HP #11577	THE STONE PRINCESS by Robyn Donald	$2.99	☐
HP #11554	SECRET ADMIRER by Susan Napier	$2.99	☐
HR #03277	THE LADY AND THE TOMCAT by Bethany Campbell	$2.99	☐
HR #03283	FOREIGN AFFAIR by Eva Rutland	$2.99	☐
HS #70529	KEEPING CHRISTMAS by Marisa Carroll	$3.39	☐
HS #70578	THE LAST BUCCANEER by Lynn Erickson	$3.50	☐
HI #22256	THRICE FAMILIAR by Caroline Burnes	$2.99	☐
HI #22238	PRESUMED GUILTY by Tess Gerritsen	$2.99	☐
HAR #16496	OH, YOU BEAUTIFUL DOLL by Judith Arnold	$3.50	☐
HAR #16510	WED AGAIN by Elda Minger	$3.50	☐
HH #28719	RACHEL by Lynda Trent	$3.99	☐
HH #28795	PIECES OF SKY by Marianne Willman	$3.99	☐

Harlequin Promotional Titles

#97122	LINGERING SHADOWS by Penny Jordan	$5.99	☐
	(limited quantities available on certain titles)		

	AMOUNT	$
DEDUCT:	**10% DISCOUNT FOR 2+ BOOKS**	$
	POSTAGE & HANDLING	$
	($1.00 for one book, 50¢ for each additional)	
	APPLICABLE TAXES*	$ _____
	TOTAL PAYABLE	$ _____
	(check or money order—please do not send cash)	

To order, complete this form and send it, along with a check or money order for the total above, payable to Harlequin Books, to: **In the U.S.:** 3010 Walden Avenue, P.O. Box 9047, Buffalo, NY 14269-9047; **In Canada:** P.O. Box 613, Fort Erie, Ontario, L2A 5X3.

Name: _____

Address: _____City: _____

State/Prov.: _____ Zip/Postal Code: _____

*New York residents remit applicable sales taxes.
 Canadian residents remit applicable GST and provincial taxes..